BLACK DOGS AND THE COLOUR YELLOW

ACKNOWLEDGEMENTS

With gratitude to Robert Edison Sandiford, writer, editor and tutor, for expert guidance, inspiration and patience. Without him, this collection would not exist.

A big thank you to Averille White for so willingly sharing her local knowledge and for hours of fun with dialogue.

Thank you also to Linda M. Deane, Hazel Simmons-McDonald, Mark McWatt, Philip Nanton, Nan Peacocke, Esther Phillips, Alake Pilgrim, Shivanee Ramlochan, and Edison T. Williams for advice, encouragement and joy throughout.

Previously Published:

"Family Home", *Poui: Cave Hill Journal of Creative Writing*, No. XIV, 2013, pp. 35-40. (http://www.cavehill.uwi.edu/fhe/LLL/poui.aspx).

"Crochet", *Poui: Cave Hill Journal of Creative Writing*, No. XI, 2010, pp. 44-47. (Written under the pseudonym Joy Murray.)

"On Being Normal", *Poui: Cave Hill Journal of Creative Writing*, No. XI, 2010, pp. 54-59. (Written under the pseudonym Joy Murray.)

"Yellow", *Bim: Arts for the 21ˢᵗ Century*, Vol.6, 2013-2014, pp.86-87. Retitled: "No Back Door." Submitted on request to *Callaloo* (with permission from *Bim*) and published in *Callaloo*, Volume 39, No. 2, pp. 630-631.

"Cut Glass", *Bim: Arts for the 21ˢᵗ Century*, Vol. 7, Nov. 2014, pp. 48-52.

"Evelyn", *The Caribbean Writer*, Vol. 129, 2015, pp. 248-252.

"He Dances", *The ArtsEtc NIFCA Winning Words Anthology, 2015/2016*. Foundation Publishing, West Terrace, 2017, pp. 14-20.

CHRISTINE BARROW

BLACK DOGS AND THE COLOUR YELLOW:

STORIES FROM BARBADOS

PEEPAL TREE

First published in Great Britain in 2018
Peepal Tree Press Ltd
17 King's Avenue
Leeds LS6 1QS
England

ISBN13: 9781845234171

Supported using public funding by
ARTS COUNCIL
ENGLAND

CONTENTS

For Jenn and Geoff, as always

PANAMA MAN

He is still young, she writes, *and strong again. He has built back his life on this small plot of land, his own. He grows corn and plantains and yucca cassava. She makes tamales for breakfast.*

Their little girl runs to him; he swings her high into the air. She shrieks and chatters like the birds of their forest.

At night, they dance – his quadrille first, then her salsa. His hand on her hip finds her rhythm. Her dark hair shimmers down her back. She wears a full-skirted red dress and black shoes with gold buckles. She rolls his name over her tongue, "Frederico." His eyes light up, he throws back his head. His cry of freedom echoes high above the canal, over the dark hills of Panama, across the Caribbean Sea to the small island where he was born.

She rests the pencil on her green notebook and sits very still. *Maybe a blue dress,* she thinks, *the silvery-blue of the butterfly that watched over me.* She removes her glasses, tilts her head to put drops into her dry, stinging eyes, and straightens her stiff fingers. She grips the edge of the table as the pain rips up her back, sends its needles through her bird-bone ribs. She knows it well. *Enough for tonight.* Tomorrow, God willing, she will continue as much of his story as best she can.

The rain outside smells like dead leaves. The screech of crickets and tree frogs seems louder than ever.

————

Some months ago, Maggie had fussed and fretted as she dealt with all her mother's things. First the bathroom cabinet – tossing the half empty bottles of Alcolado Glacial and jars of Ponds vanishing cream, the twisted tubes of Bengies Balsam into a large black garbage bag. She threw out candle grease, coconut oil and brown

bottles of pills – the bitter pills of Mama's long torment; her hair
dropping out in strands, then chunks; curling up against the
agony, and more agony. And the bawling, "Lord, take me home."
A lifetime of suffering, truth to tell – her own mother dead in
childbirth, her sense of abandonment always there in her too-
tight hold on her one daughter.

In the bedroom, Maggie emptied out the dressing table, the
chest of six drawers and the closet stuffed with dresses, shoes,
handbags, hats with black bows and net veils; multicoloured
crochet shawls, gold-plated earrings, a gilt cross on a chain. She
shoved everything into cardboard boxes, ready for The Salvation
Army. Maggie hated to throw away anything – just in case – and
she didn't fancy butting up on someone in church wearing one of
her mother's dresses. But it was more than that. There was a
reluctance she didn't understand – as if she couldn't deal with the
ending, all the unanswered questions. *Foolishness*, she chided, *as if
Mama's clothes could tell you anything.*

Maggie put on the kettle to make ginger tea to soothe the pain
in her own chest. She would have to make more effort. It
wouldn't do to leave the boxes for Keith, busy in Washington in
his big new embassy job. She lifted her eyes whenever she
thought of him, her son, reaching so high. And for the blessing of
Keisha, his thirteen-year-old girl-child, living with her. *All us old
people should have someone young to love – young and fresh, and full of
good health. Thank you, Father.*

In the front room, she made a start on the desk drawers full of
paper: the Christmas cards, funeral service booklets, bookmarks
with tassels and tracts from the Bible. *Like Mama never threw
nothing away.* Once she'd found the title deed for the land, the rest
could pelt out. But she found herself reading everything, thinking how little she knew of her mother's life. Every day, the couch
was strewn with frayed, yellowing pieces of paper. Is this all that's
left after a life lived?

One evening, she came across the envelope from Panama,
hidden between a bunch of old receipts held together on a rusty
metal prong that was attached to a block of wood. Inside were a
sepia photograph, punctured through the eye, and a letter.

October 20 1907

To my little sparrow

I hope you are well. Obey your mother and say your
prayers. Do your schoolwork good and remember your
reading. The work is hard, but the Lord does provide. I
coming home soon, God spare life.
From your grandfather
A. D. Brathwaite

Maggie caught her breath. *He wrote to me.* It took all her
strength to pull out the drawer and tip it upside-down on the
floor. *What had Mama done with the rest?* But she found nothing
more.

She smoothed out his punctured eye and put him in a silver
frame on her bedside table. His face was out of focus with no
expression, like an old ID picture. But the photo showed his high
forehead, flared nostrils, ears that stuck out a bit, and a protruding
bottom lip, stubborn like hers. There was a deep scar across his
cheek she'd never seen before. Through her tears, he blurred into
two faces, two pairs of eyes avoiding hers.

*Grandpa, you used to carry me places in books on evenings –
Wonderland and Fairyland. When I cried because Mama got vex with
me, you would hold my hand and say, "Come, let's fly away on a magic
carpet," or "ride a white horse with wings". I could be a white rabbit
out of a black top hat or a princess waving my silver wand to make
anything happen.*

*Me on your lap, turning the pages, your strong tobacco smelling like
burning sugar-cane.*

Except on a Friday, when you went out with your friends and
I would lie awake late, waiting for you to come home. You would
belch and curse when your foot hit the front step or your head
crashed against the door frame.

She hadn't really thought about him in donkey's years, but his
words had always been with her, guiding her – "respect yourself,
be true to yourself."

Grandpa, why did you leave me?

He began to trouble her, just so, as she was washing the wares or seasoning fish, hanging out Keisha's school uniform, or clipping back red hibiscus. When she was dusting his books, his face – turned sideways, never looking at her – broke into her thoughts. *Lord, give me peace*, she begged. Though she paid him no mind, he was there again on afternoons when she was trying to rest or concentrate on the crossword.

How could you come back here, confusing my head after all these years? You were everything to me – grandfather, father, brother, uncle. You left me behind, your one grandchild, and you promised to come home soon. "To my little sparrow". You forgot my name? You forgot me?

She turned his photo face down. When that didn't work, she shut it in the drawer of her bedside table. Still, he hovered in her dreams.

———

Maggie sat on a high stool at the sloping wooden desk in the public library and turned the heavy pages of an atlas. Maybe if she knew more, it would settle her mind. She traced the route from Barbados across the Caribbean Sea until her finger touched Panama and the great canal. She borrowed history texts and copied details of hardship, sickness and death into a blue notebook she had bought specially. It had a thin black ribbon for marking the pages.

Roosevelt let no obstacle stand in the way. I took the Isthmus, he declared.

But she also read that Panama money sent home had bought food and school shoes, wooden boards and shingles to replace those eaten out by termites; new galvanise to fix roofs and palings. And land. *He must have sent money to buy this house spot, the very same one, week by week by week. Mama never said a word.* Maggie let her glasses slip down her nose and stared over them, trying to control her breathing.

Grandpa, did you use to open up your jalousie window on mornings and look out from your patch-up, patch-up, two-roof wood house; rust-

eat-up galvanise, prop up on groundsel block, holding up against pelting rain and hurricane only by the grace of God, to your one goat, two-fowl and breadfruit tree?

Were you like all the others coming to visit their children' mothers, because they could never afford to be man in their own house and put food on the table; afraid their newborns would die before they could walk, or grow up with potbelly, scaly skin, ulcers oozing pus on their legs?

And you got that feeling in your belly, dreaming about freedom – and your own-own land?

Maggie was at home rocking in her cane-bottom, mahogany chair, calming her nerves when Keisha rushed in from school. "Gran, what's the matter?"

"Nothing, dear. I was thinking about your great-great-grand-father."

"I'm going to netball practice. OK?"

"Back before dark." Maggie squeezed Keisha's hand. "I'm making fish-cakes and bakes."

She busied herself in the kitchen, shredding the salt-fish soaked since morning, chopping thyme, onion and hot pepper, sieving flour and baking power.

No matter how much Maggie prayed, her dream kept coming back – the dream of black-edged envelopes with Panama stamps falling through her letterbox, one after the other, like a pack of cards, the image so vivid, it remained when she woke. Unanswered questions followed her like a shadow, troubling her spirit until she felt she had no choice.

———

"Hi, thank you for calling Tony's Travel. My name is Rashida. How can I be of assistance?"

"Good morning, Ra… Rashida. My name is Veronica Margaret Beckles and I am calling for information on travel to Panama."

"Yes, ma'am. We offer cruises. Honeymoon special package on now – fifteen nights. Explore beautiful, exotic places: Cartagena…"

"No, I just want to go the Panama Canal."

"Canal's included, then Costa Rica, Guatemala, up to Mexico and…"

"No, I want to stay at the canal, go to the museum at the canal."

"Well, you still got to fly to Miami, then take a Copa flight to Panama."

"How much is the flight?"

"When are you planning to travel?"

"July…," during Keisha's school holiday when she would be with Keith, "for two weeks." That should give her enough time.

"Return?"

"Well, yes."

"Single?"

"No, I said return. I have to come back."

"Ma'am, is you alone travelling?"

"Yes, of course. Listen, miss, I will call you back."

Maggie heard the muffled suck of teeth. "Thank you for calling Tony's Travel. Your business is important to us. Have a nice day."

She sniffed. Young people of today – too fast and fresh. And why must they make it so difficult? Copa, Carta, Costa – wherever they are. She opened her notebook and wrote: *Passport application. Suitcase. Doctor's appointment – extra painkillers.* And she might need something to help her sleep. If she could sleep well at night, she'd be fine.

Little by little, month by month, Maggie saved her meeting-turn money and whatever she could from her pension, tucked away in the drawer of her bedside table, next to his photo.

————

She looked all over for it. Only last week, she'd held it as she prayed for guidance. She must have put it somewhere safe, somewhere she should remember. But no, not in the locked desk drawer with her ticket and passport, not in her carry-on, or the Ziploc bags with her medication. He'd given it to her on her tenth birthday – the perfect pink shell, the size of an egg – in a white cloth bag; laid it beside her bowl of Cream of Wheat. "To keep you safe, sweet child," he said, and left for Panama.

From then, she'd never been without it; carried it in her

schoolbag, her shopping bag; put it under her pillow at night. You never knew what life could bring, if your prayers would be answered. So, she held it between her hands, against her ear; stuck her tongue into its whorls, and recovered from the flu, chicken-pox and dengue fever. Plenty times it kept her safe, like when the mad, black dog got into her yard, and a rat the size of her foot into her kitchen. It got her through when Keisha was born and after Keith went to America. She'd squeezed it so hard when Mama took forever to die that a piece broke off. *What did you expect?* She scolded as she glued it back together. *It wasn't meant for that.*

Now she searched in every drawer and cupboard, under sheets and towels, beside shampoo and lotions, behind plates and pots. Maggie had never thought of herself as superstitious – she would walk under ladders without a thought, and directly in front of black cats. Yet she believed the shell was some kind of charm, as if a small part of her grandfather's spirit was coiled up inside, ready to protect her every time she needed him. *Nonsense*, she told herself. *You could as well drop a cup and hang the broken handle over your ear.*

Maggie made herself look around her front room. Everything was in its place: the desk with the photo of Keisha and her netball team on top, the couch with blue crocheted cushion covers, the cabinet with her glassware neatly arranged, the shelves with his books all upright. Even the thin layer of dust on the small table beside her, and the dead fly on the windowsill were familiar.

But her eyes kept straying towards the two suitcases on the mat by the front door, packed and ready to go. In all her seventy years she'd never left home and Panama was so far away – one thousand, three hundred and eighty miles. Flying through Miami more than doubled the time – four hours to get there, then wait another four, and another three more to Panama. Keith had organised the flights, booked accommodation at a rainforest resort, and paid for everything.

To her great relief, he insisted that Keisha go with her. "At least, you got to be safe," he said. His way of caring, bless him. She'd even agreed to the wheelchair – she was so terrified that he'd come home and see how brittle she looked, thin as a thread fraying in the wind.

Giddy bubbles burst in her chest as if her spirit was telling her to fly, fly away. Or maybe warning that she was too frail, and too late. *You foolish old woman, you should have gone six months ago when you found the letter.* What if she and Keisha got separated in those airport crowds of pushy people? What if she lost their passports or fell asleep, and they missed the flight from Miami? What if she got really sick?

Maggie's hand strayed across her chest, to her left breast, then her right. She rolled up the sleeves of her blouse. Her arms looked even more withered, as if bone marrow was sucking in flesh, turning her inside out.

She started at a sudden thought and hurried into the kitchen to the fridge's freezer compartment. Behind the two ice trays was the white cloth bag – left there when she'd fixed Keisha a glass of lemonade. Maggie clasped the freezing shell and spun around the kitchen table. She blocked all dotish thoughts from her mind.

———

In the dimly lit museum at the Miraflores Visitor Centre overlooking the canal, Maggie and Keisha peered at blurred photos of men drilling, blasting, digging, dredging, hauling, and dumping excavated material. Glazed eyes stared as if to another horizon as they queued for wages, for health checks, for porridge slopped into enamel bowls; or lay gaunt on hard hospital beds with bars.

"*More than 60 million pounds of dynamite used every year,*" Keisha read. "*Every day more than 600 holes drilled and blasted… 153 million cubic metres of earth and rock from the Culebra Cut.*"

Keisha entered *Brathwaite* in the museum's database. "Gran, what was his first name?"

Maggie shrugged, "I only know A.D."

"What about Adolphus? They have two of them."

"1905. Could be."

"Oh no. Look, 208 men called Brathwaite in here. We'll never find him." They moved on. "Gran, listen. *They came from many places and spoke different languages… bringing with them nothing but their desire to work and their hopes… gave their lives for the project.*"

"All hope and glory, then," said Maggie. What she saw was men covered in mud, crawling over rocks like crabs, their faces too unclear to see or imagine any likeness. He'd been one among thousands – anonymous, expendable to those who never knew him.

"*Most came from Barbados,*" Keisha said. "*They started families, made fortunes, and exalted the country.* Gran, can we go now, please?"

Outside on the balcony, they stared in wonder as the gates eased open, thick grey water swirled around the locks, and a massive container ship swept through the narrow concrete waterway. "The engineering feat that marvelled the world," the commentator drawled into a microphone. "Gigantic aquatic elevators raising the ship up fifty-four feet." Maggie imagined him down in the deep pit digging and shovelling, trudging with chunks of rock in a box on his shoulder, clambering over landslides and falling, deafened by dynamite blasts. Maybe he had stood up to his stomach in the slimy, infested swamp with a can of DDT on his back, pumping with his right hand, spraying with his left, as the white man beside him, in his white suit and hard hat, dipped a white plate into the water and picked out squirming mosquito larvae with a suction tube like the one for her eye drops, only much bigger.

Grandpa, what happened to you? Dynamite blow off your foot? Landslide bury you? Snake poison you? Mosquito bite you? Night-time chills and sweating – you stopped taking the bitter medicine they gave you? Pneumonia from putting on clothes wet and cold from the day before?

Maggie gripped the balcony railing to steady herself. She had pressed a red hibiscus flower from her garden between the pages of her notebook, planning to lay it on the water of the canal. But she was too far away.

––––––

Keisha gulped her Coke as they sat waiting for the coach to take them back to the resort. "Granny B, you sure I can't get you anything?"

"No, thank you, dearie. I'm fine." Maggie took a small package from her bag and unfolded the white paper napkin. Inside were two small corn tamales wrapped in banana leaves. "One for you, one for me."

"Gran, you took them from breakfast!"

"Yes. And don't look so shocked. You are too young to meet hard times – don't know a thing about making do."

As Keisha ate, Maggie opened her blue notebook. "Now listen, child, I have something to tell you. Your great-great-grandfather, he would have signed a contract. Five hundred days of labour starting the day after he reached here in Panama. Ten hours a day, eight cents an hour." She turned the page. "He had to be a 'silver' man, so he got paid half what the 'gold' white man got. And by the time they finished the canal, more than twenty-five thousand men were dead. From yellow fever, malaria, cholera, tuberculosis; from dynamite, being buried under avalanche. Exploitation! Slavery supposed to be done long time, but it come back worse, killing men like him."

At Keisha's silence, Maggie regretted her stark words. She took his photo from between the pages of her notebook. "Look, love, I don't know how he got that scar. I don't know what happened to him. My mother, I used to ask her, but she would never speak about him. Never – like he never was."

"Gran, you think he had another family out here – children?"

"Keisha, it's not everything we can talk about. One day you will understand." Another stab of pain made Maggie's head reel. She grabbed Keisha's arm.

"Gran?"

"I just need the ladies' room. Help me up."

Maggie leaned over the basin and splashed cold water on her face. She held her head in her hands and refused to look in the mirror. She knew too well what she would see – her yellowing pallor with dark shadows under her eyes, neck hanging in dry folds like a turtle's. Everyone had warned her. Doctor Brown: "My dear, such a long journey. I wouldn't advise it…" Father Paul: "If you must, Sister Margaret. God be with you." And Keith, shouting on the phone: "Mother, please, at your age? What kind of madness this is? The man dead and gone, long time. And why you didn't discuss it with me first?" He'd gone on like this, until he'd realised there was no changing her mind.

The Lord had never tested her with more than she could bear, but now she wasn't so sure. What if she died here? What about Keisha? And Keith? He was right to call it madness. Her life-light as fragile as a candle flame, how could she be so selfish?

———

Maggie's first thought as she woke was that she'd come safely through another night. She reached under the oversized white pillows for her shell, still doing its best to keep her safe. *Thank you, Grandpa.*

She looked across at Keisha, sleeping – her mouth soft and slightly open, one brown arm raised over her head. Fuzzy wisps of hair had escaped her tight braids; the pink beads were her mother's idea. *A teenager now, her periods come and her little breasts, the time when a young girl really needs her mother, but that woman spent her time at the gym in skintight tights and gold trainers, or gallivanting off shopping in New York.* Tell the truth, that whole confusion and the separation between her and Keith had really bothered Maggie. But he never talked about it, so she knew to keep her thoughts to herself.

Her prayers had been answered. Keisha was the sunshine of her life. It hurt too much to think about not being there for her, through her growing-up years. But she'd already told Doctor Brown, there was no way was she going through any cutting open, cutting out and stitching back up, like Mama had.

She was never one to lie around in bed. Bed was for when you were sleeping or sick. She swept off the sheet, flexed her cramped fingers, stretched her legs and rinsed out her dry mouth. Still in her long white nightdress, with the high neck and sleeves buttoned at her wrists, she sprayed insect repellent on her hands, put on socks, threw her shawl over her shoulders, bent to kiss Keisha's forehead, and tiptoed out to the patio.

———

The early sunlight rose behind faraway, dark, forested hills and shimmered a golden path across the river towards her. She held onto the patio bars and lifted her face to its warmth.

Grandpa, you ever watch this morning miracle?

This land was strange to her. An hour ago, everyone at home

would have greeted the same sunrise with plenty noise and cafuffle – dogs and fowl-cocks, goats and black-belly sheep, bicycle bells and car horns, children's laughter and neighbours calling to one another. Here, there were no houses, no roads, no people, and no animals dotting the landscape. Just endless, empty silence – the past hidden underground in the bones of men who had taken their stories with them.

The Lord must have created this sacred place, she thought, and hidden it away from the sin and suffering of mankind, like a great nature cathedral, so that we could come here to refresh our souls.

Grandpa, you ever let this cool stillness calm your spirit?

It began to pour heavily and Maggie hugged her shawl. Rainwater trickled through the grass and around the reeds into the choppy, black river water. It would gush on to the Gantun Lake, mix with the sludge of the canal, surge over the locks and escape into the ocean to make waves and more waves, to melt into the sparkling blue Caribbean Sea.

Keisha bounced out, waving the cellphone Keith had sent her for the trip. "Daddy just called. He wants me to buy him a Panama hat. He said to say, 'Hi'."

Said to say, 'Hi'. So, he's still vex with me, Maggie thought as she eased herself onto one of the patio chairs. "Good morning, Keisha."

"Sorreee. Good morning, Grandmothaah." Keisha slumped onto the chair opposite. "I told him they were made in Ecuador – the hats." She stopped, still for once. "He's always telling me how I should be with him, but I'll miss all my friends. And you, too, Gran. Mostly you."

"Maybe you should think about going. I can come and visit you." There was nothing Keith wouldn't do for his sweet girl. Maggie knew he would carry her to live by him when…

She looked away. Moments like this were too much to bear.

Keisha jumped up and pulled down her panties. "Look, mosquito bites on my ass."

"Keisha!" .

"Gynormous lumps on both cheeks."

"Bottom, backside, even botsie or bumper, but not…"

"Go on, Gran, say it!"

———

As they walked through the rainforest, Keisha imitated their Spanish-speaking guide's pronunciation of the 'oh', 'née' and 'ka' of Veronica. Maggie especially liked the rolling 'r'. "And my name is Alicia. My other names: Herrera, from my mother, is a name from Columbia. And Chong from my grandfather – he is Jian Lin Chong. He come from China, for build the railway. He run away and they find him. Send him back to China. Then he come back to Panama. Now I want go China, meet my other family."

Maggie pictured trails of men crisscrossing the world – from Barbados to Panama to China, like ants marching over an enormous, sugar-coated net. Women everywhere losing their fathers, their children's fathers, their sons – all of them leaving home and making new families far away. And all those children left behind.

Flamboyant birds whistled as they flitted between the trees. Maggie's fascination grew as she recognised them from the tour brochure – the tanagers, motmots, caciques, toucans, woodpeckers, ant wrens, squirrel cuckoos, hummingbirds, hawks, herons and more. *How come the Lord created such brilliance in this dark forest, and could only make blackbirds and brown sparrows and wood-doves for our bright sky at home?* A large blue butterfly followed her. Its wingtips were black with what looked like fine stitching. *Blue Morpho, male, big as my hand.* When she stood still, it perched on a leaf and, as she walked on, took up its position over her head.

"He smelling you, sweating," Alicia said. "And this is the plant women take. Boil it and drink, if they don't want have the baby. Is call the God plant. Crazy, eh?" She swept the sole of her boot across a bed of small leaves that folded at her touch. "Sleeping plants."

"Whoa, I know them. Touch-me-nots." Keisha clapped her hands. Her exclamations – "Awesome" and "That's like... so cool" and "Oh my God" – made Maggie frown. She would have to speak to her again, but today was her treat. Let her be.

The canopy of trees blocked out the sky, the breeze, trapping the humidity. Maggie lagged behind. "You two go ahead. I'll wait here," she called. Her head was on fire and her heart fluttering, as if she had swallowed the butterfly. Her blouse was soaked, the back of her neck stiff and aching, her bag heavy like never before. Raucous howler monkeys hooted from the trees, their stench overpowering. Vultures hovered overhead. Birds screeched and flashed multicoloured streaks across her eyes. An army of black cutter ants blocked her path. She slipped and grabbed a branch. There was a rustle in the bush beside her. An iguana ready to jump on her? Or a snake come to crush her?

She was sure that the blue butterfly sensed her terror as it circled above, drawing her on an invisible thread into the clearing. It was once an Indian settlement, according to the label on the wooden bench. She sat under the shelter of palm leaves woven together, and waited for the bad feelings to pass.

————

A barefoot old man stumbles towards her and slumps onto the ground. The dim light of the moon casts a shadow around him. There is mud between his toes, beneath his nails curled under like the beaks of old parrots. His knees protrude through his rolled-up khaki pants; his shoulders stick out through a torn shirt that used to be white. The frayed brim of his mash-up Panama hat hides his face.

She wears a black robe with gold embroidery around the neckline. On her lap she holds a tamarind rod in one hand, a notebook open in the other. It is a dark red notebook. "So, what you story is?" she demands. "It different tuh all the others?"

She stands and faces him. "Answer the question, man. Why you lef' home? Hard times? No money? Rab land, no food?" She slaps the rod against her thigh to the beat of her words. "Malaria, smallpox, cholera, dysentery? You tell the plantation, nuff o' this suffering, go to hell? You tell them that?"

She takes three strides towards him, shouting, "Or was you bewitch by lies and sweet talk 'bout free passage, easy work, go home when yuh like? Money hanging from trees like golden apples? You did listen to the foolish bragging from them Colon diggers come back with gold teeth? See them strut and swagger?

Watch them roll silver coin on the ground for children to ketch? That crazy Panama itching all you men got in you blood, it take over you mind, too? You and you friends in the rum-shop slamming dominoes, slapping one another back and hollering, 'Come lewwe go, lewwe go Panama'?"

She can't tell if he's breathing, but she has come too far to stop. "You hearing me, Panama Man? Or you deaf? Dynamite deaf?" She paces around him. "Tell me, you spree out the rest of you money? You too shame to come home broke? The women here confuse you with them Spanish ways? You wear them charm? Join in revival meeting, speak in tongue, get possess with them spirit? Marcus Garvey put fire in you? Mek you fight and get slash 'cross you face and leave that scar? Or you gone down, down, ketching hell – poor, peaceful and polite? You call that betterment?"

He lifts his right arm over his bowed head, finger-bones splayed as if to tell her, *Enough*. But she has more. "And then you remember all o' them brek-down, one-leg, one-eye, stagger-home men? Yuh hear them song:

Fever and ague all day long, at Panama
Wish you were dead before very long, at Panama."

She turns the page of her notebook. Her voice is quiet. "And when you too sick and wear out from working double-shift, them dump you on the stinking streets of Colon, no way home? Them spit at you, chumbo? Flies buzzing in you eyes, vultures flying 'round, and you lying in the gutter?"

"Where them rest you bones in this hellhole? A stranger say a prayer for you?"

She returns to her seat and lays the rod on the ground. She closes her notebook. The man raises his eyeless sockets, toothless gums. He shakes his head. He has no answers for her.

Maggie grabbed the arm of the bench until she stopped shaking. She took a large white handkerchief from her bag and wiped her eyes, her forehead, the back of her neck. She looked up and reached her hands towards the blue butterfly still flitting over her. *Dear Lord, give me strength, guide me back where I belong.*

She heard the girls' laughter ring out.

———

Before dawn on their last day, Maggie walked through the deserted garden of the resort, past the ornamental lamps and swaying traveller's palms, her feet sinking into the soft, wet ground. Lightning flashed across the horizon. The thunder clapped loudly enough to upset the rhythm of her heart. But her heartbeat was strong again – no palpitations, no shortness of breath. She held out her hands – no shaking. She swatted at the mosquitoes whining around her ears. "My blood too thin for you. And it going poison you," she hissed. "Bite me and is you going dead!"

As the wind stirred ripples across the Chagres River, her red hibiscus floated towards the canal. *Lord, take it to his spirit, and the spirits of all those men, wherever they are.*

Maggie bowed her head for her own appeal. *Father, you already gave me my three score and ten and some extra to come to Panama. Meaning no disrespect, but please for more time. I will have the chemo. I will take the injections and swallow every one of the pills, remember my eye drops every morning and evening, and I will eat three times a day. I promise to be at service every Sunday morning and bring the boxes with Mama's things for those in need. Lord, I am begging you, just a few more months before you take me home.*

I will buy a new notebook, dark green like these hills, to write his story – what I found of it in the museum, the forest and the canal – to leave for Keisha for when she is ready to understand.

Then I will tear up his contract and take him by the hand away from all the hard labour, the danger, the fever, and the loneliness of his five hundred days. We will fly far away from the dead-grey canal, over the dark green forest, to the blue Pacific coast. The sun will burnish his sallow skin, the rain wash away his scars and cool his fever, golden corn tamales will nourish his bones. I will hold the pink shell to his ear until he hears birdsongs again.

I will give you a new name, Grandpa. And a new family. No one will ever find you.

HE DANCES

So here you are, dressed down for another of his performances, like you can't help yourself. He backed away when you reached to touch his shoulder. He looked right through you as you gave him your go-for-it thumbs up. And yet, you stay?

You rub the lenses of your thick glasses on your oversized yellow T-shirt and blink around the auditorium, buzzing and filled to capacity. You take your seat in the back row and wait. You remember how he used to dance, loved to dance, all kinds of dance. All you had to do was clap your hands, and he'd be jamming, wining, prancing – anything from classical ballet to Caribbean folk to electric slide – just for you. He danced in the playground, along the beach and over the waves; on his bed leaping to touch the ceiling with both hands, legs outstretched like an arrow in flight. He was never still: head bobbing, shoulders swaying, toes tap-tapping, slender fingers playing on the edge of his school desk. Even his eyebrows twitched up-down to the music in his head – drumbeat and steel-pan clang, violin and saxophone swing. Teachers told him, "Focus, concentrate," and threatened lashes with rulers. The nurse, checking eyes, ears, teeth and fingernails, hollered, "Jeez-on boy, sit still, nuh?" And the doctor, "Keep your tail quiet, do," when he got a little nail-jook or a plimpler of wood in his toe, dancing barefoot. His mother said he was forever springing up, like the one coil of his hair that would never lie down no matter how well she combed it into place. His father told them all, "Let the boy be."

Now you see her, that girl, in a skintight, off-white dress, an artificial yellow flower stuck behind her ear, walking to the front row – reserved seats. That girl who pushed her force-ripe self between the two of you, always there like a screeling mosquito;

and you became the hanger-on. That night at Club Extreme, her last ruthless stunt. He stopped his gyrating, clinking fork against empty beer bottle, and gaped as she bewitched with her own dance. Bashment in red lycra and black plunge top, no bra, no shame. On his lap, bubbies push up in his face, she kissed him full on – the only time you saw him still. The slut with the pouting bottom lip and squint in one eye.

"Like she's looking over your shoulder for someone else," you told him.

"The only girl for me," he told you.

"Wait for me," she told him when she left to study in New York for three years.

What about me? you wanted to say. Didn't you get it? He no longer threw his easy boyhood arm over your shoulder. When did it stop being brotherly love for you? Don't you know it's hopeless? Listen to the voice of reason in your head.

The doors close; the audience sits back, hushed, with arms folded. You see the choreographer in the wings point to the corners of his eyes and lift his fingers – *look up;* open his arms – *embrace the audience; they'll each think you're dancing only for them.*

You know the sign language.

The dance begins – a duet. His partner's emerald-green leotard is bright against her high-brown skin; he is darker, the same colour as his tights. He looks naked, his chest like polished mahogany, toned, hard, untouchable. Is this why you're here again, loser?

Raised together, same age; you were like brothers, only he was taller, fitter. But that didn't seem to matter then. His home became your home when your mother went to England and left you behind with your great aunt and her burn-in-hell strictures against every unnatural abomination. You were there when his mother put a book on his head and he twirled around like it was glued on; and when his two older sisters bound him to a chair, blue school tie around his waist, skipping rope binding his ankles, pink ribbons his wrists, and he squirmed free as if he were shedding his skin, while you remained locked in yours.

His father was like a father to you; slapped you on the back, a

man-to-man hug, as he took you to Billy's Bar to celebrate your
barely-pass BSc Management. Shot after shot of rum, with a
knockout punch. You were sick as a cow with gastro, but you
knew he loved you, too, as you are. No disgust in the curve of his
top lip. "Be yourself," he smiled. He never compared you with his
son. Not like you did, sad sack with your plastic-laminated certificate and your shadow-life shame burning in your belly, while he
had everything: father, mother, sisters, the girl, the applause – and
the perfect body – the body you love to ogle. Yours flourished fat
like a pile of worn tractor tyres while he grew from knockkneed,
bony boy to lean, sculpted thoroughbred – dancing.

That was before cancer got his father and his sisters lost their
high spirits, his mother her all-things-beautiful songs, her heartache stitched up in the long seams of her black dress.

And you with your short-sighted attempt to cheer him up.
"You remember when your dad…?"

"I can't think about the past," he said.

"You sleeping OK?"

"I dream about her," he said. "She should be back soon."

"We need to talk," you said.

"Nothing to talk about," he said.

You hurt then, and saw the opportunity to hurt him, to spit it
out. Instead, you held onto the frayed thread between you. *Let him
find out about her for himself.* Is that what you were thinking?

Tonight, you see the hang of his head, his heavy pace across
the stage as if his grief weighs down the soles of his feet. Yet he
dances well enough, keeps time with the drum. But it's the green
dancer who's the star, he the back prop. She skips, leaps; he holds
her high over his head. "As if she's a hummingbird," the choreographer told him, pointing. "Position your feet so." He swings
her over his shoulder. He's learnt how to make it seem effortless,
though now it looks automatic.

These days, he dances as if he has to, as if he's dragging himself
through a rain cloud. You know he does it to escape the paper-
pushing emptiness of being trapped behind a glass-framed counter in a grey uniform with a National Bank pin on the lapel,
working to help his mother make ends meet by counting out

other people's money with an air-conditioned smile. You know he is dancing for his father, to keep his memory alive, to imprint his look of pride, unshakeable, even as his one boy-child dropped out of school to dance.

He sets her down on one foot, the other high in the palm of his hand. The dance is over. She bows to scattered applause and holds out her hand for him to come forward. He looks towards the back row, his unseeing gaze rolls downward, across the audience. This is hardly *embracing* them. You hold your breath.

He sees her. And freezes.

You guess a super charge explodes in his heart, zips through his veins to burst through his eyes. You see him opening his arms, launching into the air, soaring and twisting like a dark kite tugging to pop the cord. The whole stage is his. His feet stamp and kick. Hips move like hot oil. Sweat pours off his forehead and chest. The drum picks up his rhythm, pounding faster, calling up his father and his father's father, for all his ancestors to rise and hold him high. He dances as you have never seen him dance before – for her, the girl he waited for.

Your heart beats in your ears. You struggle out of your seat and wave your arms, your sign for him to slow down, stop. Don't do it for her, she's not worth it. You're the one who went to all his rehearsals. You helped him up when he fell. Only you have seen his blisters and bruised black toenails. Only you know about his cramps, shin splints, heel spurs, torn Achilles tendons, about popping painkillers. "Like women," the choreographer smirked. "Don't stay on one brand too long."

Still he dances, darts and spins in a frenzy, until he can dance no more. He sinks onto one knee, his hands flat on the stage, head bowed. Jaws have dropped; hands are clasped in wonder; the audience is transfixed. The back rows, the middle and front rows rise like a tidal wave, roaring, hands clapping over heads. He stands, his arms unfold, gentle now like an animal flower, fingers quivering.

Tears stream into your open mouth.

He sees her empty seat. He runs offstage. You stumble after him, watch him limp outside on burning feet. You hold back.

At the far side of the car park, he sees them, walking away. He knows that hand draped over her shoulder. You know it too. It is the hand that pointed: *Position your feet.* The hand that gestured: *Look up.* The hand that reserved the front-row seat, now sliding down her back and opening her car door. You hear the voice, as he must have. "See you later, Babe."

You should have told him.

The audience is calling him. The green dancer grabs his hand, pulls him back inside and pushes him forward, centre stage. They cheer and whistle. Someone shouts for an encore and others pick up the call. They sit forward; every eye is on him. You hide in the wings. You wipe sweat off your face with your yellow T-shirt and replace your glasses. You are close enough to see the tremor of his bottom lip. You can feel it. You did try to tell him – yes, you did. And now you want only to protect him, as he protected you back then, when the school bullies geared up, nudging each other and flicking their thumbs in your direction; and he would step in with a comic dance until they cracked up with laughter and went back to their footballs and marbles, and forgot about you.

You know he has nothing left in him. But, yes, you silently plead, *Dance now, brother, slow and cool. Dance for yourself.*

ON BEING NORMAL

Step on the wire…

Once, long, long ago – before you all were born – in a small village on an island far away, there lived a young fisherman and his wife. Anderson, better known as A-man, was strong with a big heart – don't mind the easy-boy smile. They said he used to be own-way and had a temper that could blow like one of them Soufriere volcanoes. He wasn't no sweetbread. But all that changed after he met Amy. She was a fine girl with a complexion like brown sugar, a sprinkle of freckles across her cheeks, eyes bright like tamarind seeds, and an extraordinary sense of smell. Just like her grandmother, people said. She fell in love with Anderson – he was the onliest man for her. The two of them lived loving, and soon she was expecting their first child. Their happiness was complete.

But happiness is a not an easy thing; it could pass and go, just so. In those days, people believed that happiness, like all good things in life, should share out more or less even. No one was entitled to more than their fair portion. If you had good fortune, you had to play it down since, as anybody could tell you, after the pride comes the fall. But Anderson, like he couldn't help it. He walking 'bout the place bigging-up himself like a dog with ten tails. Lord have mercy, what was he thinking? So, looking back, it wasn't so much a surprise that their son was born not quite normal. He had webbed feet.

Towards the end of her pregnancy, Amy was tormented by dreams of fish and crapauds big as her head. Now she knew why. She gently spread open his little toes like a fan, and screamed. Miss Ophelia, the midwife, pressed her index finger to her pursed lips. Anderson, who was pacing outside the bedroom door, must have thought it was the last and sharpest scream of labour.

Miss Ophelia assured Amy, "Don't mind the feet. He going grow up good. Babies born so, them blessed with good luck."

And so it was, for a good while.

They christened him Marc after Anderson's father, though Amy was doubtful – bad enough his toes were marked, without naming him so. But she consoled herself with the thought that no two babies were born the same. Some were blessed with good looks and high-brown complexions; others were bright, or had fathers with money and a wall house. Some could swing a cricket bat like Worrell, or dance and sing all night like Jackie Opel, or give you a joke and tell a story sweet, sweet. Even those that had nothing – only rags and shame – before you knew it, some godfather would see their promise and lift them up. All you had to do in life was find your talent and make the best of it. And Marc had plenty talent.

Amy's heart glowed as he turned over and sat up before other babies normally did. He was the happiest of children, and the special way he had of babbling non-stop and holding on tight-tight to their fingers made everyone love him. She leant over his cot as he slept, filling her lungs with his milky sweetness, and her heart with a fierce protectiveness she had never felt before. She counted out his ten toes, her little finger stroking the soft, translucent skin between them, like butterfly wings. But she kept them hidden; covered them up, in little booties and socks, which seemed real odd to most people, in all that hot sun. But she got away with it. Anderson had no idea.

For true? Yes, my dears, you could well ask. But, you know, fathers beforetime were not like how fathers are today. They didn't bathe or dress their children, not even their sons. When they tried to help out, the mothers would fuss. "Careful now, not like that. Hold the head so. Come, lemme show you." Babies were women's business and the men held back.

Only occasionally would Anderson frown and tell Amy, "Stop humbugging the boy, nuh. You too like to smother him." It was well known that over-mothered boys grew up spoilt, or worse, developed unnatural ways later on in life, to their fathers' deep and everlasting shame.

Amy's plan was to wait until Anderson's love for his son grew so strong that nothing could shake it, before she showed him the child's feet. She held her breath and watched as he bounced Marc on his knee and crawled across the floor to amuse him, barking and whining like a big black puppy-dog. Anderson gazed in wonder at his son, the product of his seed, the pride of his life, the son that featured him in every way. "Look, he even got my forehead," he shouted for all to hear as he paraded Marc through the village. He meant high brow, since people back then used to think that was a sign of intelligence. When Marc walked for the first time, at eight months, Anderson lifted him into the air, shouting, "My boy, my boy!" That same evening, he brought home a new brand pair of boy shoes, blue with red laces. Like they used to say back then, Anderson was in goat heaven.

Amy braced herself. She smelt her secret frothing up like yellow scum in a stinking drain. Tomorrow she would tell Anderson, or maybe next week. But the weeks came, and went. And, as you all know, the Lord does like to move in mysterious ways. Maybe He had given Amy plenty time. More than enough?

So one evening, He send down the rain and her whole world crashed. Listen now, I will tell you how it happened.

Amy always had Marc ready for bed, in his one-piece sleep suit with enclosed feet, when Anderson reached home. But the rain – bucket-a-drop! – had her running late. She was out in the yard taking in the washing, and Marc still had on his day clothes, and the laces in his new shoes got knotted up. Anderson sat down, lifted his son onto his knee, untied the knot, eased off the shoe, and gasped. He yanked off the other shoe and staggered to his feet. His chair fell backwards, knocking over the side table, and the family photo of the three of them in a glass frame smashed onto the floor. Marc fled behind the couch. Amy, who had her nose buried in clean white sheets, ran in – fast-fast.

"That," Anderson hollered, glaring at Amy and shaking his finger at the couch, "that is NOT MY SON."

Well, well, well. As you would understand, Anderson's denial ripped Amy's heart open. She knew how men could be, how vital it was for their children to be born normal, or better still perfect in body and mind – especially a boy child, and the first one at that. She knew about fathers who lost their reason and blamed the mothers for damaging unborn babies by falling down carelessly, or eating the wrong type of food, or looking at pictures of big-belly children with malnutrition. Even worse was when they cursed the very same mothers for stepping out and going with other men. But, cuh dear, everyone knows that babies are born as God made them, and all that stupidness ig'rant people used to do, like pulling up the baby nose-bridge and shaping up the head, could not work.

And, let me tell you, plenty children looked nothing like their fathers but, mostly, the men accepted them and raised them as their own – no shame in that. But some foolish fellas used to send their own mothers to check out the babies' features and, sad to say, sometimes if they didn't like the baby mother, they would refuse to own the child. Like the mechanic fellow living down by the shop, when his son was born with a sleepy eye, he got on stink: "Not in my family!" Idiot man, out and gone he was, left the woman sooner than you could clap your hands and say, *prax, palax.*

Anderson was not that kind of man. He must know for sure that she had never even looked at a next man since they were going together. And how careful she had been during her preg-nancy – didn't eat too much of the fish he brought home and made him chase that stray duck out of the yard, quick so. Now she sensed his old bad-john self was coming back, his temper hotting up red. She blamed herself. Well yes, you could say that she should have told him right from the start. Whatever might have happened then, could never be as bad as this. But dear, oh dear, how was she to know?

From the day of his outburst, Anderson ignored Marc and cut his eye at Amy. Not a word – not one word. When she tried to talk to him, he shrugged her off like a dog shaking water out of its ear. He whistled through her pleas and turned up the Rediffusion. He cut himself off from everyone – no more the village handyman fixing up people bicycles, pan-carts and jalousie windows, or making kites and guttapercs for the boys. Done with all that, he was.

On evenings, he would come home and cock up his heels. He ate his food as usual, but then dressed down in a flashy shirt and went out. Amy's tears soaked into the very same shirts as she pressed them. Pairing up his socks, she pushed her hands inside and held them together in prayer. "Please Lord, bring my Anderson back to me."

She lay awake at night, clutching his pillow to her breasts, remembering how his sweet-eye smile used to wrap around her like a loving vine, and how his own special scent played on her heartstrings. After he bathed on evenings and got rid of the fishiness, he was like mature mahogany wood after rainfall – on mornings, like sweet molasses.

It was late when she heard the kitchen door slam, his heavy footsteps across the wood floor, and the creak of the couch as he slumped on to it. She bent over his snoring body and scrunched up her nose at the stale stench of rum and smoke and sweat. But there was no hint of cheap, trashy scent – nothing so. At least, she could be thankful for that.

Amy had a special place in everyone's hearts. Her smile sparkled like sunshine on sea water and made them forget their daily trials and troubles. And her sense of smell had saved many of them. Yes, my dears, she could sniff the air and tell you if rain or high wind coming, so you could lock up your doors and windows, and tack down your roof. She would flare open her little nose-holes, breathe in, frown for a second, and call out to her longtime friend next door, "Veda, check the pot, rice burning." Or ask the diabetic woman sitting next to her in church, "Granny D, you get you feet check recently?" And once, she was boldface enough to say to Reverend Franklyn, "Excuse me for asking, Father, but when last you had you blood pressure take?" You would never believe it, but one morning she smelt smoke from a kerosene stove clear across the gully and raised the alarm. All kinds of disasters – amputations, heart attacks, tooth cavities and extractions, burnt food and burn-down houses – were prevented, thanks to Amy's sense of smell.

As they saw her lose her spirit, the village women exchanged looks with one another, especially with Veda, the same burn-rice

Veda. They prided themselves on being different from the lick-mout' women who liked to get into other people business. So, they held back, waiting for Amy to catch herself and work her own special charms to draw her husband back to her. But things got worse and their worries grew.

"See how she fall 'way," said one, "how she dress drooping down?"

"Dragging she feet like she shoes got in mud," said another.

"Hair looking like a cobweb."

"And cry-water got she eyes red, red," said Veda. She missed the noises that had echoed through the cracks between the boards of the house – the mother singing baby songs and telling Anancy stories, the boy's footsteps tap-tapping, the father's laughter and, later, the muffled sighs – sounds of family living that were only noticed when they no longer happened.

Now, you well know, and they did, too, how it is for a young woman without good loving, a young married woman, too besides. They noted her absence at church and knew that Reverend Franklyn had counselled prayer and patience, and a return to the fold. Be that as it may, after more than two months, they figured it was time to talk sense into Anderson, to take the same kind of action their own mothers and grandmothers had taken, back down through the years.

The strategy, though not exactly subtle, had always been effective. Led by Veda, they made their visits on evenings shortly after Anderson reached home, no more than four of them at a time. They sat around Amy's kitchen table, skinning up their faces and talking loud-loud about the foolishness men believed as regards paternity and pregnancy and childbirth. They told stories of how fathers shunned their children born with club foot, yam foot, finny foot and parrot toes; even one, idiot-poppet, whose son had an extra toe sticking out right there beside his little toe. Their language got more crude and rude, and their cackling more raucous – one set of noise and cafuffle. Amy smelt the danger, red as jumbie-bead poison, and she tried to shush them. But they were older and wiser, and she respected their judgement.

Stubborn, hard-ears Anderson refused to change his don't-carish ways, don't mind he could hear every word. So, the women moved on to the next stage of their plan. They engaged the services of Miss Ophelia.

Miss Ophelia had arrived from a neighbouring island – so long ago, no one could remember which one – and had delivered hundreds of babies. But babies were scarce since the family planning nurses were handing out pills, tying tubes, and pushing coils and loops up inside, and telling women to have children *By Choice and Not by Chance,* and that it had nothing to do with God's will. So they were having only one or two babies – and mostly the men couldn't understand what was going on.

And so, Miss Ophelia diversified her talents and her risk portfolio. Yes, my dears, you would probably call her an entrepreneur these days, ef yuh please. She became an expert in healing the whole set of ailments that affected everyone at some time in their lives: nail-jooks and plimplers, burns, worms, head lice, chinks and chiggers, fresh colds and lying-in colds, gas and bad feels. She also knew exactly how to deal with the vexation and botheration between men and women. She was much in demand and saved plenty men from boiling water, and plenty women from a mob-o-ton of blows.

In two twos, she had moved from her little two-by-four with a shed roof to an upstairs wall house and put a sign on her front door.

Madam O. St. Rose
Expert in Sickness and Health
(and all Feminine Afflictions)

Sometimes, around the village, you would hear comments about low island people and their nancy ways, how they like to come here and fool people – like the same Granny D suffering from sugar that went to see her because her husband was always quarrelling and carrying on. Miss Ophelia sold her a bottle of clear liquid. "Take it and hold it in you mouth until he quiet, then spit it out," she said. Poor old Granny D never did realise she spent all that money on a bottle of standpipe water to shut up she own mouth.

Tell the truth, though, most people were frightened of Miss Ophelia, 'fraid she would put something 'pon them. In those old-time days, I telling you, they believed in all kind of foolishness – duppies and baccoos and steel donkeys and the heartman – so, mostly, they kept their remarks to themselves.

Be that as it may, Miss Ophelia turned up at Amy's house with a jar of greenish-coloured liquid. It smelt like dead cockroaches mix up in dirty pond water. "Put three drops in he food, every evening," she said, "no more, no less."

So said, so done, though as you can well imagine, under any other circumstances Amy would never dream of doing any such thing – never, ever. But she was desperate. The poor girl had tried everything – even gone so far as to put on her wedding gown and greet him at the door one evening and then stripping off in front of him. Another time she dropped his empty plate, and fell to the floor as she bent to pick up the pieces. But, as she lay there, Anderson stared over her as if she didn't exist, not one flicker in his dead-cold eyes.

After two weeks of three-drops-a-day and no change in Anderson's behaviour, though he ate every mouthful of his food, Amy's doubts were confirmed. The potion was to tie your man and that was not her problem – the said thing she'd been trying to tell Miss Ophelia all along. Anderson wasn't no womaniser; she'd smell it on him if he was. And he wasn't no rummie, neither – well, not really.

A few months passed, and it seemed to everyone that Amy was just not able. As Veda said, "If not for Marc and having to feed and bath him, she wouldn't know if it was day or night."

They didn't know how much her own madness was troubling her – the wedding dress and her striptease, the broken plate and her fake fall. There was only one thing left for her to do.

One morning, Amy asked Veda to mind Marc and walked the four miles to where Zena Skeete lived. The following Friday evening, she took Marc to spend the weekend with her mother, in town.

If you ever met Zena, you would never forget her. She was a cob-skin woman with fine straight hair, tall and hale, upwards of six-foot, and she moved like the moon sliding out from behind clouds. Her front teeth were small and sharp like broken glass, her finger nails painted bright red, and she inked in her eyebrows so they looked like a frigate bird in flight. Mothers threatened to take their bad-behave children to Zena for her to cut off their back-talking tongues, or put them in her big black coal-pot and boil out the wickedness, and sometimes eat them up, too.

Zena would peer at you as if she could see right into your soul and, when she was vex, which was quite often, she rattled off in tongues nobody could understand. It was said that she could turn into a ball of fire at night, and that she used special ointments to keep herself tight-tight down there, so that it would fit smooth and silky, but could squeeze like a vice, when necessary. Mostly, she kept herself to herself. People knew where to find her, though, and she was never known to refuse a request.

It was near midnight when Zena went to look for Anderson. We will never know what she did. He, himself, might not remember much and, anyway, no way would he ever say anything to anyone. But the neighbourhood women saw her enter the house and stayed up to listen.

"Nuff noise, like fowl cocks 'pon a morning," said one.

"Tree frogs whistling," said another.

"Nah, more like pigs."

"All that grunting and groaning, like crapauds doing it."

According to one woman, a bat with enormous wings and blood dripping from its claws flew out of the bedroom window. But some people will say anything.

No one said a word to Amy, not even Veda – certain things not even close friends could tell one another. When Amy and Marc reached home on Sunday evening, there was an odd mix-up smell like dead jellyfish and burnt cane, but she said nothing.

Signs and wonders! From that night on, so the story goes, Anderson was a changed man, not foolish-foolish like some men when Zena was done with them, but back to his regular self. He lifted Marc onto his shoulders, held his bare feet, one in each hand, and carried him 'round the village.

Anderson and Amy lived together happy for the rest of their lives. They were blessed with another son who, according to Amy, smelt like warm butter biscuits. Whether his feet were normal or not, we will never know, but Anderson accepted both his sons as his own and loved them dearly. Only Amy could sense that Marc was his favourite, as if he had a little making up to do.

As for Amy, well, my dears, she gradually lost her extra-sharp sense of smell. But she didn't mind that. Tell the truth, it was a bit much, what with all the diagnosing and forecasting she was expected to do.

And Marc? He grew up to be a real nice boy. He played cricket as well as the other boys and swam faster than any of them. When they called him *Fin-foot*, he grinned and returned the compliment – for all boys have nicknames, to remind them that they are all the same, no better or worse than one another.

The wire bend. Story end.

THREE, TWO, ONE

Eleanor's long shadow is sharply outlined on the concrete ahead of her as she strides along the Careenage, swinging her string bag and humming a reggae tune. She's running late. But there's no one at their table. She huffs; it wasn't her idea that the three friends should meet at the Waterfront Café, every Saturday.

She slips onto one of the three upright seats under the green awning. They have elegantly curved, wrought-iron backs, painted a lighter green. The man behind her, inside the café, watches as she arranges her strands of ebony and silver beads threaded on strips of leather and pats the braids coiled around her head. She lifts the hem of her ankle-length black dress to just above her knees and stretches her legs and arms, like a dancer embracing the day. Men are attracted, and challenged, by her style. Alan, though, seems to enjoy simply being with her. He lets her be herself, and she lets him know when it's time to leave. She needs her space.

A message from Tamara appears on her cellphone. What now?

———

"Hi, Ellie. Sorry, yoga finished late." Michelle is decked out like a frangipani flower – bright yellow Capris and a white top with cap sleeves. She kisses Eleanor on both cheeks and points to the copper wire ring with a jade-coloured stone on her left thumb. "Oh, I do love that."

"Oh, no, you don't. You've seen it before and you know it's not real."

"Right. Sorry." Michelle fluffs up her damp curls. "I'll just go and freshen up."

Eleanor sighs and looks out at the row of white boats at the water's edge. *Fancy Free* and *Sunshine Girl* bob and bump against one another in a tipsy dance. She sways her shoulders in rhythm.

Michelle returns and sits opposite with her hair perfect, make-up on, and her brave-face smile. Eleanor knows it well and shifts to their schoolgirl talk. "So, chile, you goin' good?"

"Fine," says Michelle, but she's replaced her smile with a downward-facing yoga-dog look.

"And you?"

"I here – hangin' in."

"And flirting, as usual."

Eleanor's eyebrows shoot up. "Me? No way. Guide's honour." She holds up the three middle fingers of her right hand in salute. "The man looking good, dough, nuh? Check the biceps."

Michelle refuses to look. "How is Alan? It's him we need to check, Tammy and me. She's coming?"

"On her way. And it's only been two months. I don't know him myself yet."

"So?"

"So, he came over last night."

"And?"

"And nothing." Yet not nothing. Last night, Alan sitting on the broad coral-stone windowsill of her studio, with the rum and water and slice of lime she'd made the way he likes it, pretending to read the newspaper, but glancing across at her, at her thighs gripping the wheel, her right food pedalling, her tongue over her top lip, her hands around the lump of soft, slimy clay, slender fingers stroking, squeezing and lifting, thumbs pressing down inside. Shaping the pot – a slight wobble, then perfect symmetry.

He'd raised his eyebrows in mock-fear as she pulled a piece of wire taut between her fists. She slid it under and cupped the pot in both hands, laid it on the workbench as if it were as fragile as a bubble. She gave him an elaborate bow, holding up her hands, dripping clay.

"Come here," he said, but it was he who went to her, opening his arms, muscled like those of a man who lifts weights, not one to hook up with a string bean like her. She knows that he won't wait too much longer.

But Eleanor is not ready to share this, even with her best friend. So she asks, "Where's Zoe? I thought you were bringing her."

"Confirmation classes."

"But it's Saturday."

"Extra…"

"What?"

"…early start."

"She's five years old, for Christ's sake!"

"Richard insists."

"Ah, Richard. Pillar of the law and now the church. What would this country do without…"

"Ellie, stop. Please." Michelle is blinking rapidly. "I'll go and get the waitress."

Eleanor blows out her cheeks. Shite.

———

The three have been friends since primary school. Each an only child, they were not the cleverest, nor the prettiest, just together like fledglings in a nest, covering up for each other with fingers crossed behind their backs, sharing every one of their little secrets, and the coconut bread, tamarind balls and sugar-cakes in their lunch boxes. When they all passed for Queen's College, the best secondary school for girls, they held hands and shrieked.

"We did it," said Eleanor.

"Unbelievable," said Tamara.

"Together forever," said Michelle, "like sisters."

They'd held tight, the only three to go to school by bus, country bookies up against town-girl sophistication. Tamara was chubby and flatfooted, hopeless at netball, and struggled with proper English; Michelle was shy, with freckles and a lisp. But Eleanor was the tallest girl in the class, shoe size six. No one dared mess with her and her friends.

They cried together through monthly cramps and acne zits; invented their own secret code of knowing looks and hand signals, and often fell about in helpless giggles, like the time they imitated their science teacher's toothy outburst – "This one takes the biscuit" – after Tamara blew up and burst a paper bag during an experiment. They were Girl Guides together, though Michelle chose the Cook badge, and Eleanor the Craft one, but they both did First Aid. Tamara's was something to do with conservation. One badge, she said, was good for her, a green one. Michelle always liked yellow best, and Eleanor the deep tones of mahogany and indigo. "We're like a rainbow," Michelle said.

They didn't really notice when they no longer caught the same bus home.

———

"She's coming," says Michelle.

"Who?"

"The waitress – made me feel like a real nuisance."

Eleanor shrugs and passes her phone across the table, showing Michelle the message from Tamara – st andrew bus late c u soon.

"What's she doing out in St. Andrew?"

"Me nah know. Mussee a next man." Eleanor's voice softens. "Miche, what is it?"

"Nothing... nothing I can't cope with. It's just every day. You wouldn't..."

"Try me."

"Every day, school runs, karate and piano lessons, tennis and ballet..."

And confirmation classes, Eleanor thinks.

"...and maids and gardeners and plumbers."

Collecting his wigs from the dry cleaners.

"Tempers and tantrums, every day. And Zoe's crying a lot and wetting her bed again. And the boys don't speak to me unless Richard's there... Sorry."

"And Richard?" Richard, above it all, another bewildered man wondering what could be the matter with his wife. What more could she want?

"He's really busy at work." Michelle's voice rises. "Ellie, I keep telling you, Richard is a decent man. He's never cheated on me." She looks down.

Richard – his very name triggers recoil in Eleanor. Big-shot lawyer. Queen's Counsel at thirty-something. The world his courtroom. 'Absolutely' – his favourite word. SMS, Eleanor thinks, small man syndrome. She'd met him just before the wedding, but already knew too much about him – how he'd wangled custody of the twin boys from his first marriage, be-witched Michelle with diamonds around her finger and neck, got her to put her career as a going-places auditor on hold, gave her permission to have one child, and made her wear flat shoes. Could I, Eleanor asks herself, have found something to like in him if he'd married someone else?

He has it all planned. He will rise to become a high court judge, receive a knighthood – Sir and Lady Richard Harding. His power play; her sell out – that's how Eleanor sees the set-up. And Michelle knows it.

Eleanor knows that whatever's upsetting her friend is not children or chores.

"There she is," Michelle says. "Look, or rather, don't. And I'm alright. Don't say anything." Eleanor groans as Tamara waves, trips and grabs the edge of a table. She hugs Michelle who wrinkles up her nose, and puts her arm around Eleanor's shoulders for a quick squeeze before slumping onto the seat between them, facing the Careenage. She taps her fingers on the table. "Made it. Have you ordered?" Typical, Eleanor thinks. Over an hour late and no sorry; nothing so.

Michelle tries not to look at the new tattoo of a scarlet heart with barbed wire around it on the back of Tamara's left hand. Eleanor sees that two of the fingernails on her right hand are broken – one black, the other green. Why is she wearing a plain white shirt, buttoned right up, so unlike her usual plunge neck-lines? And why the large, black lens sunglasses?

Michelle smiles her hyped-up smile as she reaches to tuck in the label at the back of her shirt. "What were you doing in St. Andrew?"

Tamara flinches.

Michelle sits back, but chatters on. "Remember when we went there on that school outing, and I sat on those turnovers…"

"He beat me," Tamara says.

"...cherry jam all over the seat of the bus, what a sticky... What?"

"Who?" Eleanor asks.

"Dwayne, last night. He laughed, like he would never stop. He said if he didn't laugh, he'd have to beat me some more."

"Who's Dwayne?"

"No matter. We done, finished. I need a lawyer." Tamara looks towards Michelle.

"Oh, um, but Richard doesn't do..."

"I've got to get a restraining order."

"Tammy, are you hurt?" Michelle holds her hand – the hand without the tattoo. "You saw a doctor? Called the police?"

The waitress's high heels clack as she approaches. She places cut-glass salt and pepper shakers and three white paper napkins on the table. "Hi, guys, how y'all enjoying this beautiful day?"

"Like hell," Tamara grunts.

"At last," Michelle murmurs.

Eleanor cringes. She won't be here for long; too much attitude. And those heels.

"We got fresh juices – mango, guava, golden apple."

"Three coffees, please. One decaf, two regular," Michelle says. "And bring the bill."

Eleanor points her finger at Tamara. "You can't expect Michelle to get Richard involved. She's got enough on her plate." She feels a kick under the table. "Anyway, you need a female lawyer."

"It's alright, I'll ask him." Michelle takes hold of Eleanor's finger. "But where will you stay? You're not going back there?"

"Where else can I go?"

Michelle looks down and shuffles the salt and pepper shakers around the table. Eleanor is focused on removing a speck of clay from under her thumbnail. Tamara stares out over the water. She's still wearing the sunglasses, but flicks her head as if she's trying to shake something out of her eye. "Ugh, I wish those boats would stop moving. I need to sit where you are," she says to Michelle. She stands and her seat tips over, wrought-iron clanging on concrete. She grabs one of the napkins, holds it to her mouth and stumbles into the café. The man inside half stands as if to help.

"Oh, sugar, what are we going to do this time?" Michelle says as she pulls the seat upright. "Her breath smells stink."

"Call a taxi for her." Eleanor twists her ring around her thumb. "Listen, I don't want to meet here anymore."

"How can you say that?" Michelle pauses. "There's something I should tell you." Eleanor leans forward. "About when her mother died and she stayed with me." Eleanor closes her eyes. She thought Michelle was going to talk about what really has her upset.

"It was awful, like she couldn't cry. Locked herself in the bathroom, always bathing, bathing, as if she was trying to scrub herself away." Michelle's eyes fill. "The man her mother was seeing abused her. They never found him."

"Jeez, I never knew."

"She made me promise not to say anything. Anyway, you were away."

I was away, Eleanor thinks, in Jamaica. Off to Art College, finding myself, and never looking back. I'd mastered the art of sidestepping Tammy and her problems.

"Ellie, she only has us. That's why I thought we should meet on Saturdays."

"Haven't we done enough for her? Are there no limits?"

"Right. Bad idea. Sorry, sorry. OK?"

They are silent as the waitress places three coffees, milk, sugar and the bill on the table. Michelle is fiddling with something in her bag, probably her phone or her watch. Eleanor lifts her gaze across the shimmering water to the Chamberlain Bridge and the Parliament Buildings. She stirs sugar into her black coffee. "Miche, I know how you feel, but…"

"You know nothing, Madam Got-It-All-Under-Control." Michelle looks down and a fat tear drops onto the table. She sniffs back the rest. "I'll go," she says.

Eleanor reaches out and touches Michelle's arm. "My turn."

———

Eleanor remembers the time at school when she told Tamara, "Go ahead, mess up your life, see if I care," though she can't recall

exactly what it was about. She herself was busy reasoning with the
Debating Club girls, spurning prescribed topics, like "A Good
Education is a Passport for Life," in favour of "The Bussa Slave
Rebellion" and "Back to Africa with Garvey." Michelle hung on
longer, as best friends should, not giving up on Tamara, but
staying clear of her force-ripe group with their foolishness about
cute boys – "who going wid who and who get dump" – and their
disgusting sex talk. Michelle spent hours in the library, studying
really hard; and her new friends initiated her into the posh QC
walk and talk, their two-cheek pecks, mwa-mwa.

She blossomed into the special kind of girl the school was
designed to create. So they both lost track of Tamara's detentions
for rudeness and her suspension for truancy – though she was
given a second chance, "on account of issues at home." They
couldn't believe it when she hissed, "I hate you two," and dropped
out of school the week before her sixteenth birthday.

After years of drifting from shop-assistant to waitress to babysitter,
Tamara found her voice, her soul voice. She wore locks, head-ties
and earrings with beads and feathers that dangled to her shoulders;
lost weight and changed her name to Folami. Her audiences at
open-air concerts were mesmerized as she darted like a firefly
against the night sky. With picnic baskets of canapés and rosé and
arms draped around each other's shoulders, they swayed to her beat,
moved to tears by her songs of solitude and betrayal, loving her.

Loving her, until one night her emaciated body, dripping bling
under multicoloured lights, could take no more. She fumbled her
words, lost her way across the stage and fell, leaving her fans
transfixed between shock and applause. Those in the back rows
cheered, thinking it was all part of her act.

Eleanor and Michelle agreed they should have been there.
She'd sent them free tickets, as always. Guilt followed them
like a shadow, bloated with the endless gossip they heard
delivered with malicious glee. "I hear you friend gone and get
sheself in trouble again." They dried her out and revived her spirit
as best they could.

But there was no persuading her to return to the spotlight.
Tamara quit – her own light snuffed out.

Eleanor stands inside the café, trying to steady her breathing as she watches Michelle finish her decaf; she's put saucers over the other two cups. She answers her cellphone, retrieves her watch from her bag and looks at its oval face with four Gucci diamonds. Eleanor knows she keeps it hidden to avoid her comment.

The man is still there. He catches her eye, but Eleanor turns and rejoins Michelle. She puts her elbows on the table and covers her mouth with both hands. A braid falls across her cheek. Michelle moves next to her, to the seat Tamara had occupied.

"She was slumped on the floor," Eleanor says, "hugging the toilet. Her foot was blocking the door. I couldn't get it open."

"Oh, God, I should have come with you."

"I had to call the barman. We got her up, out the back door, into a taxi. He said they'd clean up the mess."

"Mess?"

Eleanor mimes vomiting with her hands. "Her shirt buttons were undone. I saw the bruises on her neck. She kept calling for her mom." Eleanor wipes her eyes with the second napkin. "She's gone to pack her things. I told her she can stay with me."

"Oh, Ellie." Michelle uncovers Eleanor's coffee and slides it towards her.

Eleanor holds up her hands. "For a week." Only a week, but would Alan understand?

Almost a year ago, Eleanor had surprised herself by renting a building in the plantation yard of a Great House, owned and occupied by a family that could probably trace its roots back to slavery. But it was ideal with two storeys – three bedrooms upstairs and plenty space for a studio below. Whitewashed coralstone walls, cool with high ceilings, and a view of the sea across the cane fields. She was determined to keep herself to herself and declined the family's invitations to sundowner cocktails, until the three little grandchildren, two girls and a boy, peeped in at the jalousie window, inched through the door, and charmed her. She arranged seats for them next to her workbench.

Eleanor's ceramics have won awards, but she keeps her trophies stashed in a cupboard and likes to tell people that she just potters about. There's nothing she enjoys more than to have Zoe come over and watch the four children play together, rolling out clay and coiling pots, or folding coloured paper into humming birds and flying fish to thread on strings and twirl around. With little hands covered in clay, paint and glue, they stroke each other's arms and hair with curiosity and delight. The easy way all children make friends, Eleanor muses.

――――――

"Ellie," Michelle clutches her bag and rocks forward. "Ellie, I putht him off me, last night." Her lisp is back.

Eleanor clamps her lips between her teeth to stop the shout bursting out of her: Yes, finally, you told him. No!

"I told him I had a terrible tummy ache. He knows I was lying. He's never looked at me like that before... like judgment." Michelle strips the cuticle off her index finger with her teeth. "I don't know what made me do it. God, what's wrong with me?" A small bead of blood appears. She dabs it with the third napkin, licks her finger and dabs again. "What will I do if he leaves me? And takes Zoe?" She folds the napkin over the two red spots and puts it in her bag.

Eleanor clasps Michelle's hand. "He'd never do that," she hears herself say. But he's done it before.

"I can't live on my own. I'm not like you."

Like me? Eleanor freezes. She lets go of Michelle's hand.

"And I was going to ask him about going back to work, now Zoe's at school."

Eleanor doesn't trust herself to say anything. She makes herself think about Zoe. Only last Saturday, the three of them had hunched over her first report: *A good term's work. Zoe tries hard, but must concentrate more.*

Michelle had beamed.

"Why them always puttin' down children?" Tamara said.

And Eleanor nodded. "They have no idea how bright she is."

They'd shared the joy of Zoe's first steps, her first words, her ballet – all elbows and knees, but adorable. Just to look makes Eleanor want to hug her up, clap hands and sing lullabies. She was thrilled, and speechless, when Michelle asked her to be a god-mother. "You and Tammy, my best friends. I haven't asked Richard yet, but…."

Eleanor has an idea – a long shot, but it might cheer up Michelle. "Hey, why don't you come, too, you and Zoe. We'll make lots of pots." She is about to add that they could meet Alan, but stops herself. This is no light-hearted, meet-my-friends fling. Alan has said he wants to know all of her; his eyes probe as if he reads her soul. But she holds back, and flirts. Michelle is right.

Michelle shakes her head, her smile is sad. "I have to go. He just called, to remind me to pick up Zoe. Well, that's what he said."

"But he knows you're here, with me."

Michelle flicks open her compact and checks her face. "Ellie, about Tammy, I can't ask Richard, not now. I'll keep praying for her. Call you tomorrow."

"I'm sorry," Eleanor says.

"Sorry? You? What for?"

"Me, my big mouth… about Richard."

Michelle's sunshine-girl smile is back in place. "I do love him, you know," she says. "Love you, too."

Eleanor waves her fingers as Michelle leaves. Miche, she thinks, with boundless love in her heart, despite the pain; Tammy who can't even love herself; and me, only now learning how.

———

The sky is overcast now. The shadows have blurred; the boats hold still. Across the Careenage, the buildings look bleak. Eleanor can't make out the clock tower, but hears the midday chimes, echoing Big Ben's solemn tune. Nor can she see the life-size, metallic statue of Lord Nelson, but she remembers it well, prominent as ever on a platform of concrete and marble, one armless sleeve tucked into his jacket. Her voice had been among the loudest petitioning to have him removed after Trafalgar Square was renamed National Heroes Square. But the government of the day caved in under conservative pressure and proclaimed, "Like it or not, he is part of our heroic history," and rotated him one hundred and eighty degrees further to the right. Back then, she was feisty; she said what she was thinking.

Her napkin is still damp from her tears, but she folds and refolds it into a bird, one with a long egret neck.

Four young-looking women arrive at a table on the other side of the café, flapping their hands and cackling like crazed chickens. Eleanor wonders what they're on about – zumba, pedicures, liposuction? They're not listening, not touching, not even looking at one another. Not like us, the three of us, with our three late nights – me playing with Alan in a plantation outhouse, Miche trapped by Richard in his mansion, and Tammy beaten up by whoever he was, wherever she was. So different, yet bound together, year after year, like the rings on a tree trunk. Sisters, rainbow sisters.

Eleanor stifles a yawn. She feels as if she hasn't slept for a week. She sips her coffee and grimaces. It's cold.

The man from inside the café comes over. "Hi, everything OK?"

"Yes, thank you."

"I'm Adrian."

"Eleanor." His handshake is firm, comforting.

He points to her coffee. "Allow me to get you another one."

She smiles, her own warmest smile, "Thanks, but I'm just leaving," and watches him saunter away from her along the Careenage, hips swaying, hands free. She tucks the paper bird, a new one for Zoe, into her string bag and lifts the strap over her shoulder. She hands a twenty-dollar note with the bill to the waitress who quips, "Them leave you one to pay?"

Eleanor blinks. "Their turn next Saturday."

CROCHET

Lucy is here today, as she will be tomorrow, on the patio of her mother's small wood house, from ten to midday. She will limp back out at four o'clock, dressed simply in a white cotton top with sleeves to the wrists and a grey ankle-length skirt that make her look long and pale – as if she never sees the sun. She will sit on her upright chair with the bolster cushion supporting her back, at the table covered with balls of thread in pastel colours, and stay until the shadows lengthen. She will sit until her eyes behind thick-lens glasses sting and refuse to focus, her slim fingers stiffen and her shoulders ache too much to crochet any more of the white doilies, the granny, square placemats and the yellow toilet roll covers that help to make ends meet.

This is where Lucy was born sixteen years ago and where everyone thinks she belongs. "Our own sweet-girl," the neighbours say, as if she is the lucky charm they keep in their pockets. Only at night does she admit the heartache – not so physical any more – as she lies in her narrow bed and imagines another life for herself.

————

It happened when she was eight years old, running free with games of hide-and-seek and catch-me-if-you-can through the cane field owned by Mr. Hall. She fell flat, her left foot clamped in one of his traps – a trap for rats, mongooses, stray dogs and other vermin made from the rusted springs and cogs of old tractor parts. The agony shot up her leg like lightning through wire. Her scream was silent as if she were drowning in boiling water. She didn't hear her friends call her or shout for help, or the crunch as the trap was wrenched open.

At the hospital, white-coated experts prodded and twisted her mangled foot. They deliberated on amputation and prosthesis, therapy and rehabilitation.

"Cut it off?" her mother howled. "My sweet girl, ain't she bin tru enough?"

Back at home, neighbours came with packages of sweetness – pink and white sugar cakes, tamarind balls and coconut bread. They patted the back of her hands and kissed her forehead, not looking at the bulge under the sheet that used to be a perfect foot.

"Could of happen to anyone o' we children."

"But why it had to be she?" her mother cried.

"God spare Lucy life for a reason," they said.

A week later, on a Sunday evening, Lucy heard the rattle of Mr. Hall's Land Rover, the crunch of tyres on the marl road and the manly confidence in his footsteps. She hid her crochet under the table and her foot under her skirt.

"Good evening," he said, looking over her head. She called her mother.

"I regret the incident." He removed his cork-hat. "Tell your little girl, no more trespassing on my land."

"Yes, Sir. No, Sir." Her mother stood with fists on her hips, her face expressionless. She did not invite him to sit and offer him refreshment as she did with every other visitor. She said nothing, as if waiting to see what he would do next.

Lucy had only ever glimpsed his profile as he drove his car up the front road that ran alongside the tenantry. People said that this poor-white man had come from no-place, bought up the plantation and denied tenants their rights to buy their house spots and cane pieces. He sent his overseer to collect rents every week, even during hard times.

She looked up at his clean-shaven chin and neatly trimmed hair. He smiled as he reached into the pocket of his white linen jacket and pulled out a brown envelope. As he put it on the table, his gold watch glinted in the sun. He bowed his head and left.

"Mama, what is that?"

"Hush money."

Lucy watched her mother swallow her pride at great cost while Mr. Hall cleared his conscience at so little.

———

An orthopaedic boot with a thick sole and reinforced heel had to be specially made overseas to her measurements; painkillers and lotions had to be bought, and crutches, too, and physiotherapy twice a week. A neighbour lent her grandfather's walking stick but still, the dollars in the envelope disappeared like dead leaves in the wind. They'd saved her foot, but Lucy would never be the same. Her mother's vexation calmed into resignation, her crying into empty sighs. She unclenched her fists, folded her arms and rocked herself into silence.

It took many months for Lucy to catch back herself. She began walking with her mother to the bus-stop on mornings – arm in arm, hand in hand and then with just the support of the stick. She no longer had to stop and clutch onto gateposts until the pain subsided. If she walked slowly, she could almost hide her limp. Her mother's smile stretched across her face as neighbours passed and said, "Lucy doing good, real good."

One of her evening bags, with tassels intricately threaded with silver sequins, sold in the boutique at the hotel where her mother worked as a maid. And Mistress Marshall, who owned the gated wall house on the front road, with alarms and Rottweiler dogs – a snowbird, they call her on account of her flying to Barbados every year to escape the winters – had placed an order for a belt in purple with golden beads that she would show off in New York. No more cut-and-contrive crochet; it was only a matter of time before Lucy's unique designs were displayed all over the world.

She showed off her new creations to the women of the neighbourhood who dropped in to see how she was doing, give her the joke about who get ketch t'iefing mangoes from the plantation yard and tell her who marrying, who making baby, who suffering with gastro, dengue or diabetes, and who dead. But they didn't talk about accidents or amputations – or her childhood friends jumping up in Crop-Over bands.

———

On afternoons, Lucy looked out for Damian, Mr. Hall's son. He came home late, after the other boys from the local primary school had passed – pitching marbles, jostling and tripping up one another. His uniform was different, his school private; a special bus dropped him off. He was a loner, like her, and she noticed how his school bag weighed him down, how his left foot turned inward as walked. She thought he was so beautiful with his chubby cheeks and golden curls, like a little cherub. She waved, but he never looked in her direction. No matter, she told herself, he can't pass me by for ever.

One afternoon, Lucy heard the snarls. It was one of Mistress Marshall's black dogs. She saw Damian swing his schoolbag at its flat head, bulging eyes and massive jaws and run in her direction. She dropped her crochet, grabbed the stick and hobbled into the road. The animal clamped its jaw on Damian's right foot. He shrieked – the kind of shriek that could splinter glass. Lucy kicked at the dog with her boot and clubbed its head with the handle of the stick. It let go of Damian and swung its bloody fangs towards her. She turned the stick and rammed the steel tip into its eye. It yelped and slunk away.

Lucy sat on the kerb cradling Damian on her lap. His eyes were shut tight, his fists clenched, his whole body shaking. She stroked his forehead, twisted his golden curls around her little finger and cooed from her throat like a wood-dove, as her mother had for her. She didn't feel the sun blistering her arms or see the blood on her skirt. His father arrived and grabbed Damian. The two of them were rushed off in an ambulance, siren blaring.

"You saved his life," neighbours said as they helped her home. Lucy's foot thudded in time with the beat of her heart. This was it, at last. God had spared her life for this.

———

Soon they will come visit. It will be a Sunday evening with the sky bright-bright and the breeze cool. Lucy will have her hair pinned back with two silver combs to show off her amber eyes sparkling with her new contact lenses, and her cheekbones highlighted with her mother's lipstick, just a tip. She will be wearing her turquoise skirt and matching top – the one that she crocheted with the complex gossamer web pattern. Damian will give her a

bunch of red roses and she will sign the cast on his foot with her
initials, LL, and draw a little pink heart. Mr. Hall, dressed down
in a dark suit with a yellow carnation in the lapel, will open his
arms wide-wide. "Thank you, thank you, my darling girl." But
she will respect herself and hold back.

Her mother will serve drinks on a tray, each glass on one of the
coasters she'd made in white, one-hundred-per-cent pure cotton
with tiny lavender beads. "So fine, so intricate," they will say.

Damian will sit beside her every evening and kiss her cheek and
tell her things he wouldn't tell anybody else, like how boys at school
bully him about his limp. She will put things right – tell his father
to talk to the headmaster. He will be ever so grateful again and invite
her for tea. She will say, "No, thank you," because you can't
untangle the past just like that. But he will insist, and she will
forgive. She never was one to be grudgeful.

And, in time, they will come like family, all woven together.
"Call me Uncle Charles," he will say and she will bring out his
true-true self – a good man at heart. There will be Christmas
celebrations and birthday parties, cakes with three layers and
candles, around his grand mahogany table, and outings – every
Sunday – to morning service at the Cathedral and picnics in
Queen's Park. And drives – she will wave from the front seat of
his big black car. And he will link her arm in his and guide her
through his great house, from room to room, showing her china
dishes with floral decorations, crystal glasses and four-poster
beds with lace pillow covers.

And one quiet evening when Damian is fast asleep in bed, and
they are sitting together on his gallery and the moon is full, he will
lift her boot onto his lap, undo the laces and hold her foot in his
healing hands. He will tease her at first by pulling her toes and
tickling her sole, but then he will touch her scar and rub it with
his thumbs real slow and gentle until it fades and takes away all the
pain, and the only thing she can feel is a hot tingling. And for her
seventeenth birthday, he will present her with a pair of white
patent leather shoes with silver buckles and high heels.

When Damian is old enough to understand, she will tell him
how it was with her own foot – an accident, one of those things,

could have happened to anyone, nobody's fault. An invisible thread binds them together. It won't be long now.

————

The sky hung heavy and the clouds closed in. A storm was on its way and the neighbourhood was quiet. The dog had been put down and Mistress Marshall had gone back – gone without her belt, without paying, not a blind cent. Damian had had an operation in Miami – just a standard procedure skin graft. He would run and jump as he had before. Lucy felt the dull ache in her foot creep up her leg and into her lower back. She took a gulp of the bitter cerasee-bush tea her mother had made, though she knew it would do no good.

Three Sundays had passed since the day that was to have changed Lucy's life, the day she'd circled in red on the almanac hanging above her bed. That morning she'd blacked it out with a thick marker. Her dreams had unravelled, like the tannin-stained, yellow tea-cosy she'd been unpicking to reuse the wool – the one her mother bought second-hand at her Church-of-God bazaar. It lay on the table, beside her glasses.

She knew that he would come, without Damian, if not this Sunday then the next, with his lump sum and his sense of entitlement. He would sneak a peek at her face, but he would act like her boot was invisible, that it had nothing to do with him.

She lifted her leg with both hands and placed her foot on the chair in front of her. She slipped her smallest crochet hook, the one with the sharpest point, into her boot.

His envelope was white this time, and larger. As he put it on the table, she studied his chinless sallow-yellow face, his brown buck teeth, his mean lips, his pinched nose, his hair so thin you could see his scalp. She wanted to pelt his money back at him, but her mother would hear that he'd been and she would know why.

The back of his hand was like fish scales mottled with brown blotches and red scabs. The vein that crossed from his wrist to index finger, like a blue worm, made Lucy's skin crawl. She bent forward, whipped out the hook and stabbed. She stabbed again. That time she got it.

Lucy held her breath as he stared, his mouth wide open. She stood and looked at him directly. "My name is Lucinda Layne."

His pale eyes watered with pain, but there was also shock and a flash of something like respect. He covered the bloody gash with his other hand and left.

———

By the time her mother got home, Lucy had removed all traces of the visit. She sat upright, sipping a glass of cool, pure coconut water as she tackled the exquisite pattern of a scarlet ginger-lily for a corsage, something she had not attempted before and that required all her concentration – and her finest hook.

ROOM 21B

Through the overhead air-vent in his office, he hears one of the secretaries say, "They going have to carry out Prof, foot first."

"Yeah, been stuck in there Lord knows how long," the other says and chuckles. "Like he got squatter rights."

The room has, indeed, been his for nearly forty years. Small, clean and anonymous, Room 21B suits him very well – a refuge. Or maybe a cell?

Located at the far end of the corridor, it is easily missed even by those who are looking for it. There are no windows, only the air vent with bars. The walls are white and the floor tiles beige, so that even a speck of dirt will show. His ritual as he arrives is to close the door behind him, sniff the air and run his fingertips over every surface. Only occasionally has he had to report to the secretaries: "Evidence of cockroaches, do please let the cleaners know."

There is a blackboard with nothing written on it. Above it is a white clock with a soft tick. The three-drawer filing cabinet is packed with lecture notes and minutes of meetings. More files lie in neat piles on the floor by the computer table, and on the shelf beside his philosophy books – arranged in alphabetical order by author. The desk on which he drums his fingers soundlessly, waiting for the secretaries to go away, is clear except for a plastic desk tidy that holds pens, pencils and paper clips, and a letter tray with one item – a circular announcing a seminar entitled, *Solid Waste Disposal in a Small Island Developing State*. There are no framed certificates displayed on the walls, no family photos adorning the desk. The only change he's made is to move his desk, so that, on the rare occasions when his door is open, no one walking along the corridor can see him.

By counting the twelve-by-twelve tiles, he has calculated that his office is eighty feet square – less than half its original size. The shortage of space on campus had reached crisis point and many rooms, including his, were subdivided. The Dean apologized, hinting that it was either this or double up. The thought of sharing horrified him.

————

He was in his mid-fifties when his mother died, having lingered for years, making her endless demands. He did his duty as her only child, returning to England every summer break, listening to her lament about his father who "got himself killed" in the war after he'd married her during two week's home leave – and left her pregnant.

He had more than earned his inheritance. Combined with his savings, it was enough to buy a plot of land in Bathsheba on the east coast and build his very own home. He could leave the rented apartment that still held for him the nightmare memory of the time he overdid the rum punches at the senior common room party and spun nauseously in his bed.

"Like an offbeat albino bat on tiptoe," a female lecturer said as she imitated his dance. He'd only ever learnt the waltz at his mother's insistence. It had taken him three days to recover, locked in, the ceiling lifting and lowering. Shutting his eyes had made it worse. He'd seen no one – there being no one to call.

At his office desk, with a pencil, ruler and a large sheet of white paper, he'd drawn the plan – the open-space living room; next to it the bedroom and bathroom; the kitchen behind and, stroke of genius, the patio overlooking the sea. He imported termite-resistant wood – greenheart for the walls and beams, purple-heart for the floors and fitted cupboards – and sourced rust-resistant screws and roofing material. His new home would be open to the sun and the breeze, yet with a solid foundation set into the coral-rock hillside. It would be nothing like the claustrophobic terraced house of his childhood, where the only place to hide was in the airing cupboard, curled up on a pillow on the floor, cocooned in the aroma of sheets and towels – clean, white, ironed and neatly folded.

As construction began, he withdrew to the garden where the racket of hammering, sawing and drilling was borne away by the wind. The land sloped steeply towards the sea. Already there was a grove of bamboo and several coconut palms, a tropical orchard of limes, mangoes and breadfruit and guavas as big as tennis balls. He added a kitchen garden and planted herbs, lettuce and cherry tomatoes. Sometimes he took off his gardening gloves and buried his hands in the soft, moist compost, feeling a strange exhilaration as he looked at the dirt under his fingernails.

He enjoyed the heavy physical work of clearing bush out in the open air, losing all sense of time. Yet, even as new energy surged through his body, his mind turned back to his skinny, sickly childhood, and his mother's "don't-be-such-a-pansy" treatment as he shivered with flu in the winter. In the summer, when he got nosebleeds, she'd slap icy flannels on his forehead and shove cold keys down the back of his neck.

One morning, as he was pulling weeds, he came across a natural spring. He dangled his skinny, pink feet in the cool, clear water, scooping it up in handfuls, laughing, tossing it over his peeling nose and lips cracked by the sun and salt spray, feeling its cleansing power.

"You looking for somebody to fix up the garden?" A voice behind him growled. He turned and squinted up at a man leaning against his palm tree, smoking. From that angle, the muscles of his thighs and arms looked like the branches of his breadfruit tree. Thick locks coiled around his head; he had hands twice the size of his own. How long, he wondered, had this trespasser been watching him play like a child?

"I could fix it up nice for you." The man flicked his cigarette butt into the spring and sauntered off.

His name was Rodney Boyce, who became Roddy – Roddy with the slow, insolent half-smile and menacing black eyes, Roddy who never had any intention of fixing the garden.

———

His appointment as a young lecturer in Barbados had promised a fresh start – the chance to close the door on his childhood and his mother, forget his messy fumblings at manhood which had filled him with disgust and driven him to think celibate purity was a philosophical ideal. He had tried hard to fit in and attended every committee meeting, seminar, conference and workshop, though he said nothing and thought of important points only after the sessions were over. At first, the secretaries tittered behind their hands when he said "blimey" and "gosh" and discretely suggested that yellow pants did not go with white socks, and socks did not go with sandals. They meant well, even with their silly, "You meet a nice Bajan girl yet?" and seemed to grow rather fond of him: his shyness and smiles at their chitchat – all the while revealing nothing of himself.

Everything about him was out of place – his whiteness, his accent, his urges. But, as the years passed, colleagues' appreciation of his scholarly achievements grew, though his area of expertise – the Philosophy of Consciousness – was beyond them. The Assessment and Promotions Committee had no idea how to value his six single-authored books and thirty-seven articles in refereed journals; couldn't fathom concepts like *heterophenomenology* and *supervenience*. At his retirement function, the Dean highlighted his several prestigious awards, sounding surprised, "…no idea of your global acclaim…," and his Professor Emeritus title was conferred without question. They appealed to him to continue to take responsibility for one course – Philosophy of the Mind – since there was no one else qualified to teach it. His continuing entitlement to Room 21B was assured.

Room 21A was larger with two windows. It was occupied by three young lecturers in Cultural Studies, one of whom was Winsome. "Winnie, from Jamaica," she said, bouncing into his office. One day, she'd wear a colourful, long dress; the next, a black, knee-length skirt and white blouse. She tied her hair in neat braids or let it spring out like black candyfloss. Her desk was cluttered with bright red, green and yellow knickknacks, a box of tissues, a bowl of mints and another overflowing with condoms. The posters on the wall behind her desk had bumper sticker slogans – *Real Men Don't Hit, Sisters Unite for Peace* and *God Loves Gays Too*. He couldn't help but admire her optimism.

The partition between their offices was so thin that he could hear her voice through it. Late one night, hers was more mellow than usual and there was another one. He was pretty sure it belonged to the Visiting Professor of African Literature who had decorated his office with an elaborately carved rocking chair, a deerskin rug, ebony sculptures and panoramic photos of zebras, giraffes and lions. Their grunting and moaning drove him from his own room. Much as he liked her, this really was going too far.

———

Construction of his new home was a labour of hope, determination and frustration. Masons, carpenters, electricians and plumbers all arrived late and were absent without a word of explanation. They shouted over their loud, mindless music, and refused to listen to how he wanted things done. Several planks of wood and a bag of cement went missing. And, as if that wasn't enough, Hurricane Marilyn swept away his roof.

In the middle of it all, one Saturday morning, Roddy turned up with a bundle of fish wrapped in newspaper and fried up a feast of dolphin and red snapper. The builders downed tools early and gathered on his patio – lusty fellows with big bellies, hearty laughter and appetites for life, helping themselves with fingers straight from the sizzling pan, stuffing themselves on fish cutters with hot pepper sauce.

As he licked his fingers, grease dripping down his shirt, he recalled his mother's starched white napkins, her elbows-off and sit-up-straight dining-table respectability, her self-righteous chicken-soup-book codes for living. I am what you have made me, he thought, but look at me now.

He quite enjoyed having the men stay after work, though he hadn't exactly invited them. And he didn't really mind the stale stench of fish and rum and cigarettes and sweat that hung in the air. After all, it was only one evening a week and all he had to do was open the windows, empty ashtrays and scrub the frying pan. He rather liked the way Roddy made himself at home as he sat on the kitchen step scraping scales and gutting fish, and took a secret pleasure in peeking at the long muscles of his back that ran down into his jeans, hung low and revealing the crease between his full, round buttocks. What was important, though, was their good working relationship. They complemented each other well.

But then Roddy's job as a chef at a west-coast hotel became part-time, intermittent, then nonexistent, and the fish-fry spread to Fridays, then Thursdays. Somehow, he was providing the money to buy the fish while Roddy put on a bragging host-with-the-most act for the builders. He understood little of their banter, especially since they all talked at the same time, with bloated vowels. But the jokes got more vulgar – he knew what they meant by *chossels* and *buller-men* – and the sessions went on well into the night. It all got a bit much and he felt quite put out.

One night, after the builders had left, Roddy crooned from the other side of the patio, "Come here, Mista Blue Eyes. I seeing how you does like to look at me," and grasped his shoulders, turned him around and rubbed a knee against his lower back. His pulse raced, there was a heat in his cheeks, the intoxicating odour of lady-of-the-night blossom in his nostrils. He swallowed the nausea as he fell into the humiliation he knew it would be, hearing Roddy's taunting, "Cool it, man, you like to study too much. You too blasted uptight."

Later, alone, under a hot shower, he scrubbed himself red and raw.

It took the best part of a year before construction was finished and the builders paid and gone – Roddy, too. We had nothing in common, he told himself. He was all ego and body. I was merely admiring his physique, much as a photographer would do. What future could there have been? With me as his white-sugar daddy? Cash cow? It was nothing more than animal lust. I might have become infatuated, blind, subservient, a slave to passion, like Plato said. I might have lost everything.

He loved coming home from his office on evenings, hearing the key click as he unlocked his front door, dropping his briefcase and books in the living room, stripping off in the bedroom and walking out to his patio to the brilliant pinks and oranges of the sunsets behind his home. He stood naked, arms wide open, a silent cry from his lips wet with tears, looking out to the clear

horizon and the sharp outlines of frigate birds floating free on the
wind. He was at home, at peace, at last. It was as if the strong wind
had blown away all sin and lifted a corner at the edge of paradise
to let him in.

Later, in the dark hours of the night, his mother's voice pierced
his euphoria. He saw a different image of his future – exposed on
a barren hillside amid the ruins of his home. He pulled the sheet
over his head and curled up tight around filth inside him,
knowing that the only space he deserved was Room 21B.

———

Over the years, he'd allowed himself to merge into the image of
an eccentric English professor, a shadow-man with wispy grey
hair parted on the left, bushy eyebrows and a long beard – well-
trimmed though. The secretaries referred to him as "the Duppy"
– a term of endearment, he assumed, without asking what it
meant. At precisely twelve thirty, he locked the door and sat at
his desk eating a packed lunch of whole-wheat sandwiches with
palma ham or brie cheese, lettuce and cherry tomatoes from his
garden; sometimes one of Winnie's Tastee patties, though they
were a bit peppery, with a thermos flask of mango or guava juice.
After cleaning up the crumbs, he would retrieve his walking
stick hanging from the edge of the bookshelf, put on his cloth
sun hat and head out around the campus grounds. He walked
more slowly these days, with a slight bend from the waist and
hunched shoulders, nodding to those he encountered, but
pressing on. Rarely did he vary this routine. It was what was
expected; it wouldn't do to stand out.

One Monday evening, he'd finished his lecture on the dot of
seven, as eager as ever to be home. It was raining heavily and, as
he was replacing his lecture notes in the filing cabinet, a female
student entered his office, shut the door and sat down. She was
holding a dirty, wet sandal in one hand, a dripping umbrella in the
other.

"Sorry, Prof, Sir. The sole come off." She held up the sandal.
"Yes, yes, so what's the problem?"
"Mussee the glue."

"No, my dear, not the shoe. Why are you here in my room?"

"My grandmother, she got sick last night. So, that mean I didn't get to finish the coursework."

"Quite." Recently, his response to their excuses had been loaded with sarcasm, his right eyebrow raised, though this new breed of brazen females and hetero-posing males didn't seem to get it. He turned to close the filing cabinet drawer. The lock made a loud crunching sound as he punched it in with his thumb.

He looked down at her, hair cropped short, a large glitz hoop in one ear, a stud in the other. She wore a flimsy blouse, off-white and off-the-shoulder with a plunging neckline, and a yellow skirt that reached no further than mid-thigh. As she spoke, she crossed and uncrossed her legs, alternating her sandalled foot and her wet, bare one. She'd left a clod of mud on his office floor.

He stepped back and folded his arms, ready to challenge her lie. But there she sat between him and his office door, the door she had closed. He should have told her to leave it open. He should not have called her "my dear." He should not have moved his desk. The campus took cases of fraternizing with students very seriously. Before, the men – always men, *dirty old lechers* – got away with it, or were quietly asked to resign. Now, opinion on campus had swung in favour of trollops like her, spearheaded by feminist champions like Winnie. Now there were ordinances, procedures and records; student notice boards displayed lists of numbers to call for counselling and support. Reputations built up over a lifetime were destroyed, the so-called perpetrators disgraced. He should call Security.

He reached for a file and opened it. "What's your name?"

"Tamika Jones, but my friends call me Tami." She ran her tongue across her top lip.

A record of As and B+s, a clever student – too clever. "Well, submit a medical certificate. You should be entitled to one under the circumstances."

The puddle under her umbrella was trickling towards his files by the computer table.

"Now then, Ms. Jones, you must have plans for the evening." He clapped his hands.

She shook her head, the hoop earring swinging across her cheek. "I don't got no plans." She remained seated and breathed in, swelling her breasts, reaching inside her blouse for her cellphone.

His clock showed twenty-three minutes past seven. He sat and, with his hands hidden below the desk, took a fifty-dollar note from his wallet. That should more than cover it.

"Right then, let's go." He eased past her, smelling her sick-sweet scent, and opened the door.

"You does live in Bathsheba," she said as they walked along the corridor. "I like out there." Shameless. How could Winnie support the likes of her?

At the security desk in the entrance hall, he gave the guard the fifty dollars. "Call a taxi to take her home. Goodnight, Ms. Jones."

He got into his car and powered up the engine, thinking that he'd dealt with her rather well. But he recalled the smirk on her face as he left her. By now she'd be texting all her friends. He drove recklessly. Though the rain had stopped, the roads were still wet. The slut, he thought, contaminating my room with her dripping umbrella and her mud, her stench, herself.

He showered and changed his clothes. He put three ice cubes into his favourite tall glass with that comforting clink, poured a double measure of gin, topped it up with tonic, added a twist of lime and four drops of Angostura bitters. He relaxed – at home, on his chaise long, on his patio, the glass making a wet circle on his shirt. He turned his thoughts towards the waterfall he was planning to build with the spring in his garden, and maybe a little fountain, too.

––––––––

He found himself spending more time at home, rescheduling his classes to three days a week, then two. He could work just as well from there on his laptop; easily and singlehandedly construct a bookshelf with concrete blocks and planks of wood; put his course online and get the secretaries to shred all the old files – buy them some flowers or maybe chocolates. No one would notice his absence. Maybe, he could manage without Room 21B.

And Winnie, well, to tell the truth, she had become rather exhausting, with her "reasoning", always touching him on his arm or the back of his hand with her stubby fingers. "Crikey Winnie, do calm down," he'd say as she flapped on about some injustice on campus, in the Caribbean, in the world, making him feel rather relieved at his own detachment.

And her gifts were quite overwhelming: the packets of Blue Mountain coffee, beef patties, jars of jerk seasoning and Solomon Gundy. And tins of ackee – "Cook it with salt fish, I could show you." But he never invited her to show him. And there was that time she intruded – "You remind me of my brother. He had to leave Jamaica."

A dog might be good company, he thought – a mature one, female, no testosterone, already spayed and house trained. As a child, he was only allowed a goldfish trapped in its glass bowl. His mother hated pets. "Dirty and smelly," she called them. They left hair all over the furniture and pooed on the carpets.

The blurb on the Lost and Found Canine Sanctuary's website read: *Rescue dogs are fantastic pets, forever grateful and devoted.* He scrolled through several times before making up his mind.

Name: Beauty
Sex: Female
Age: 5 years (approx.)
Breed: Mixed
Colour: Black
Size: Small.

The tilt of her head and her lonesome expression appealed to him.

The woman who rapped on his front door the following Saturday morning held a red pen and a clipboard with a questionnaire attached. "We have to check the premises," she said barging in. "Make sure our charges go to safe homes and happy families."

She ticked off boxes as she inspected her way through his living room and kitchen. "Bedroom off limits, I assume?" she asked, pointing at the closed door. Out on the patio, she wagged her no-nonsense finger. "No fence around the garden, I see."

He showed her the enclosed area outside the kitchen. "Well, I suppose we could consider a small dog," she said.

"Actually, I've already chosen her." He handed her the profile of Beauty he'd printed out.

"Have we looked after a pet before?"

"Yes, ma'am." Well, there was the goldfish.

"You live alone? No family?" The interrogation went on for three pages of ticks and crosses – mostly ticks, he noted.

"So, have I passed your examination?"

"Not my decision," she sniffed. "The Re-homing Committee has the right to disallow adoptions. Without explanation." She shook the gate outside his front door with vigour and tested the latch. "We'll let you know in due course. You'll have to sign a legal contract before you get to collect your new doggie."

He covered his mouth with his hand and pulled his top lip, but she was going on about follow-up visits, and maybe showcasing him on Facebook "as one of our success stories." He shook his head, but she didn't notice that either.

"And a donation is always welcome. The norm is one hundred dollars."

Topping the list of people that irritated him most, up there with loud, lazy builders and bold, hussy students, were bossy women with their royal *We* and their norms. As she left, he camped it up, fluttering his eyelids and waggling his fingers. Let the silly bitch think he might pervert her little doggie. With over fifty dogs on the waiting list of their Sanctuary, no way would they refuse him.

Beauty was no beauty. One eye was smaller than the other, part of her left ear was missing and she was more grey than black, especially around her muzzle. She cowered in a corner of his patio, shaking as if she would never stop. He lifted her onto his lap. "Alright, alright, my beauty," he grinned. He'd never spoken to a dog before. He examined the worn patches around her neck. "Did they bully you, too, leave you in a cupboard, shut you out?" he whispered into her torn ear, remembering the time he left his bed unmade and his mother took the sheets and blankets to the bottom of the garden, sent him out there and locked the kitchen door.

"Never mind, you are home now. Home – no more Sanctuary." He set her down on her spindly legs. She scurried into the bedroom and under the bed. On his hands and knees, he eased her out with a broomstick and a slice of salami.

He renamed her Eudaimonia – Plato's happiness. Eudie for short. Little by little, she lost her fear and thrilled him with a frenzied performance when he came home. She scampered round and round, yelping with joy, her tail spinning, making him laugh. At night, after feeding her, he lifted her onto his lap and stroked her skintight belly as her tongue lolled, eyelids flickered and closed, trusting at last.

"I see you got other company." It was Roddy, standing in the kitchen doorway, hands on hips, feet apart, leaning forward as if he were about to pounce.

————

It happened fast, so fast. He flung all doubt from his mind and made himself believe Roddy's story: "I been in Miami, working at Marriott." Cruising in years later as if it were yesterday. But it was real and it had to be right – so spontaneous. It was his last chance. And what did he have to lose?

He watched bewitched as Roddy stripped and danced, narrow hips writhing serpent-like to the drums in his head, fingers tap-clicking, dreadlocks swinging over his broad, shining back; his smell of earth and rain and sea, the potent tang of rum on his tongue, his finger beckoning out into the moonlight. New thrills of touch zipped through him like a fever. His body in spasms, he banished all taboos.

Lying on the bed after Roddy left, he laughed out loud at the two outrageous prints of hibiscus flowers he'd bought on a whim – one red, the other pink – with exaggerated yellow stamens. He preened in front of the full-length mirror, pulled in his stomach, stretched and flexed, pleased as never before with his sun-bronzed body. Mother, if you could only see me now, he sang.

Later, in the full light of day, angst took over. It was disgusting, degrading, beneath human dignity – yes Augustine, "the filth of unclean desire", "the hell of lust". He had to take control, slow things down. There must be less of the in-out, grunt and done, more stroke and simmer, more finesse.

He searched through his books. Yes Hume: "amorous passion", the synergy between beauty, sex and benevolence. It can happen for us. Loving, lasting unions are possible between all couples. Ours will be unique. The magnetism of opposites. Together we will find our own rhythm. But we should abstain for a while and share intimate feelings, our childhoods. I'll tell him about starched napkins and the airing cupboard and he'll tell me about his mother. We will build care and compassion. And love – constant, true, virtuous.

But Roddy was restless, slinking off without a word, sometimes for three, four nights or longer, saying nothing or coming up with his own stock of lies, like "My mother got sick. Had to carry she to the hospital."

He had a way of knowing when to return. When the joy of coming home to Eudie was wearing thin and long evenings stretched ahead, or after waking hot and hard in the middle of the night, Roddy would be back flashing an enormous gold watch, all disks and dials, or a tattoo of a woman's puckered lips enflamed on his neck. Asking where he got them would fall in with the games he played.

But Roddy never sat still, never shut up. Animal snorts, snores, curses and farts vibrated through the kitchen, bedroom, bathroom – everywhere. He was fed up with picking up Roddy's wet towels, sweaty T-shirts and stinking socks and tripping over his enormous sneakers. Before long, he wanted to be alone again in his home. The way to get rid of him is to ignore him, he thought.

They sat on the patio with a bowl of ripe mangoes from the garden, slicing off the ends, squeezing and sucking, golden juice oozing between their fingers. "Forbidden fruit," he joked. Roddy frowned and twisted his mouth – as if he were probing with his tongue to remove mango strings from between his teeth. It would be fine to ask him to leave, just for a while, because the dog-house woman was due for another follow-up visit.

Roddy stood, pelted a mango seed overarm, hard into the garden, and exploded. "So, you kicking me out?" He overturned the table, grabbed him by the arms, dragged him into the bedroom, tore off his dressing gown and shoved him naked in front of the mirror. "Abomination, look at you fucking nasty self." His eyes were like black bubbles, boiling. "Stinking, bad-breath, pissy old man." He spat on the floor and left.

Mango slime dripped down his beard, over the red bruises on his arms, from his fingers to the floor. The reflection of the hibiscus prints behind him mocked. He clutched at the pain in his stomach that crawled around his bowels and coiled up, like a hardback millipede.

He cancelled the woman's appointment and drove to campus, shut the door of Room 21B and leant against it. He reached for one of his publications to reread the accolades, but his books looked like his mother's recipe folders, all lined-up. The room was as small and spotless as ever, but the walls were a sickening off-white, the ceiling closing in, the window bars thickening with rust – his refuge like a cell. The clock ticked like a dripping tap. I am losing my mind, he thought.

It was late when the phone rang. "You forget 'bout the storm that coming? High wind and plenty rain. You best come home."

Home. Mine, but I've let it become his.

By the time he parked the car, gale-force gusts, and huge waves pounding up through hollows in the coral-rock were shaking the foundations of his home. He shivered and hugged his arms, the bruises turning blue but still sore, as he relived the image of it all crashing into the sea.

There was a coil of shit inside the kitchen door. He heard Roddy's staged voice, "Come, dou-dou darlin', come out from under there." It was long since Eudie hid under the bed.

"The dog must be jealous. Is he you should put out." Roddy's laugh was edged with menace.

"He is a she," was all he said.

———

The storm passed. They finished their late lobster dinner, prepared to perfection with butter, garlic and herbs by Roddy. But the only taste in his mouth was that of his mother's white fish pies and yellow custards.

Through the corner of his eye, he watched Roddy adjust the folds of the red kaftan robe around his erection; hold up his plate and lick the remains of the butter, lick his knife and flick his thumb across the blade; crack his knuckles, one by one, left hand, then right.

He was thinking about love, how philosophers had tried to make sense of love, all kinds of love, how people search endlessly for love but mess it up with sex and procreation and passion and perversion; how they think of love as natural, but there's no such thing. Maternal instinct? No, love won't just happen because a child is born. How could a mother love a child she didn't want? We have to learn how to love – and how not.

Roddy lit a cigarette and spoke through the smoke. "Why you always running off to you office?"

Not anymore, he thought.

His stomach rebelled. As he walked into the bathroom, he heard the heavy footsteps cross the wooden floor and the kitchen door slam. It could never have been love, he thought. How absurd of me to believe that. He heard the soft thud of Eudie's tail under the bed and, as he lifted her into his arms, saw the gash above her eye. That was our last supper – he was resolved. Under the cool shower, he wiped her blood away with the corner of his white towel. She licked his wet cheek.

He felt his curse begin to unravel. It would take time, but he was on his way.

SEA SPIRIT

She sleepwalks along the shore and into the cool, sparkling water. The sand is soft between her toes. Little silver fish nibble at her ankles; ripples caress her hips, her breasts. The blue-blue sea closes over her head. Now there is only the soft swish of the tide, the ebb and the flow.

A turtle glides past towards the shore. She turns to follow, but the undertow drags her into the darkness. Sea creatures swirl around her, flashing razor-sharp pincers, whiplash tentacles, teeth like needles. The current catches her, spins and throws her against sharp coral rocks. She screams, but there is no sound. She struggles for the surface, arms outstretched, feet pushing back, but cannot reach the light. She collapses onto the seabed.

A soft glow appears in the distance framing a shimmering figure in a blue-green, sequined gown. She drifts towards it. A hand, black and gnarled, but strong still, yanks her up to the surface and hurls her onto the shore. She clambers to her feet and turns to the sea. His voice commands, "Don't look back. Go, go home."

————

The old man had lived alone, beyond the boundary of the village for many years. They knew his nickname, Beak, but not much else, so they filled the gaps with old-time stories. He looked that way because a lightning flash struck him, cracked his back and burnt his skin black-black. His limp, hop-and-drop, was on account of his mother feeding scraps to a mauger, three-legged dog that strayed into her yard shortly before he was born. And some woman was supposed to have dripped sweat from her armpit into his food to tie him and it got him bewitch.

Mostly, though, they forgot about him. He was odd – selfish some said. But every so often at the North End Bar and Variety Store, someone would ask, "Wha' happen to that finny-foot fella out there?" and they would shrug, chupse and move the conversation on. Father John could have told them but, of course, the rum-shop was out of bounds for him after dark. Myra, too, but she knew to keep quiet.

――――――

Myra was only seven when her mother left for London. "To make a better life for us," she said. "Soon, soon, I going send for you," she promised on the phone. "I making everything ready for you to come."

Myra's whole life felt like one big, long wait.

She understood that money was scarce so, even if fathers were still around, mothers had to work to support their children. Sometimes they found jobs in town and came home on weekends; other times they had to go over 'n away, could be for years. So, children got left behind, with grandmothers or aunties or godmothers to mind them. Some would take it on and feel abandoned. Not Myra, though – her plan was to escape through her bedroom window one night and fly away. In her mind she could see, clear as could be, the surprise on her mother's face as she unlocked her English front door, with the big number 310 on it, to see her very own grown-up daughter standing there in the snow in red high-heeled boots.

For now, though, Myra stayed with her grandmother, where everyone said she belonged. They even looked the same way: high-brown complexion and cat-eyes – a kind of greenish colour – and their own way of walking – purposeful with feet slightly turned out, though Grandma Lou had begun to lean forward and use a cane. Myra thought she was looking a lot like a sweet-potato pudding, sitting in her stuffed and sagging easy-chair like she might disappear into it. And her allergies were getting worse. Anything – cat hair, feathers, honey, cockroaches and cane arrows – would make her go into one set of sneezing and snuffling.

She liked to pick at Myra and sometimes bawl her out. "How

you July-born people could be so stubborn and strong-headed?"
Mostly on a Sunday night when she fixed her hair for school. First
the unpicking, then the washing with soap two times, and the
towel drying and parting it down the centre, north to south; and
across, east to west; then out smaller, checking for nits.

"They like clean hair."

"Then doan wash it Grandma, please."

With Myra on a footstool between her legs, Grandma Lou
rubbed in dollops of Vaseline and castor oil with her finger,
pulled the ironing comb through – "Keep quiet or you going get
burn" – tugged at her scalp and twisted her hair into braids, all the
while humming hymns through clenched teeth.

"I want it all cut off."

"Hush, child." Grandma Lou stretched a piece of old stocking
over Myra's head and held her to her big, pudding breasts in a
back-to-front hug. "There now, it done. Off you go to bed."

She was proud of Myra, too. The girl had spirit and she was
bright, the only one in her class to pass for secondary school in
town. Grandma Lou pompasetted around the village for days,
everybody congratulating her like she was the one who sat the
exam. But lately, she was getting real fretful, her tongue sharper
than a cane-blade. "I ain' able," she told Father John. "When a
girl reach a certain age, she does need she mother to tell she
things."

————

On evenings, the North End Bar was hot, crowded and raucous
especially when tourists lost their way back to their west coast
hotels and ended up there. The men fired up their grogs and
bragged with big-up tales of how they marched in the streets with
Grantley, their wild-cat strikes as sugar-cane workers, how they
raised the Barbados flag for Independence with Dipper their
Skipper. Old, old men croaked out memories of the hell of
digging the Panama Canal and the triumph of the 1930s riots.
They toasted Frank, their own first West Indies' captain, the
magnificent three Ws middle order, and Gary's three-sixty-five
against Pakistan – not out. Raise your glasses to we heroes!

As they staggered home, late-late, mostly they had no idea if they would get let in or put out to sleep in the yard with the fowls or, if times were real hard, get cuss and pelt with hot water.

Their favourite story, repeated for every tourist gullible enough to buy the next round, was about the old man. Myra had heard it many times as she and her little friends crouched under the red, plastic cover that hung down over the table by the side door.

Two men from town had struggled to swim around the island – a bet according to some, others said they were raising money for blind people and others that it was for people whose houses got burnt down by kerosene stoves. But every one of them, and mostly they were fishermen, who well knew the perils of the sea, agreed it was crazy-dumb-stupidness.

"Them swim and swim, and swim some more," said one.

"Doan know a thing 'bout how sea could be up here in St. Lucy," said another.

"Rough, man, rough enough," they chorused, thumping their fists on the counter to the beat of "Could not make it," and shaking their heads in unison.

Here, the rum-shop proprietor took over. Selwyn "Sharkie" Greaves was a man no one would ever want to cross and plenty women liked to draw up under, don't mind his face was pock-marked like the skin of a breadfruit. Few men could remember how they got their nicknames, but his was most likely due to his wide mouth with a gold pointy tooth, no neck and sloping shoulders, and the way he had of turning his head from side to side, missing nothing. "Drag their-self out the water," he roared, "half dead, right there by where the old man did living." He paused, his audience goggle-eyed, and delivered the punch line, "When them see him, more ugly than sin, they must be think them dead-dead for true, and seeing the devil he-self!"

Everyone cracking up, laughing their bellies full. And Mistress Maizie hearing them under the table and lifting up the cover and hollering, "Out, you hard-ears little…" And them scrambling out and giggling fit to burst. And Myra, reaching home, praying, "Please Jesus, let Grandma be sleeping." Most times, she was, slumped in her chair, head lolling to one side, mouth hanging open, dribble down her chin, and Myra would put the matches or the tin of sardines she'd been sent to buy on the kitchen table and tiptoe to bed.

————

Myra had met him on her way home from school. The bus was late and it was almost dark. A storm threatened and there was no one around. As she struggled against the wind, the weirdest sound came from the sea, like the wailing she'd heard only once before, from a mother whose baby was being buried. It started like a deep groan and rose, loud and shrill, luring her down the track towards the cliffs.

A streak of lightning etched his gaunt silhouette against the grey sky. He was standing on the rocks, looking out to the horizon. His left shoulder stuck upward through straggly grey locks and his bent back protruded through his vest. He was leaning on a stick hooked under his armpit. His right foot hung withered and twisted.

"You hear she, yonder?" He turned towards Myra. "Sea spirit." His nose was like the blade of a machete. She wanted to run fast, but it was as if her feet had turned to wood.

"Good evening, Miss," he said.

After that, Myra went by him regularly, telling her grandmother she was staying late at school for extra lessons or netball practice for the under-13 team.

His hut overlooked the sea. Myra never went inside – he always shut the door as she arrived. Under an overhanging eave, there was a workbench beneath which were hunks of gnarled mahogany that he carved and polished into dolphins, sea horses, flying fish, starfish and turtles. On top, beside his knives and chisels, sandpaper, rags and bottles of oils, was the mermaid he was creating. She lay on a wave, her hair rippling across her breasts, mouth slightly open, arms outstretched as if she were offering the most precious gift. Her eyes were closed.

They sat outside, she on her school books, he on a rocking chair that couldn't rock because the ground was so uneven, and drank ginger tea with bay leaf from enamel cups. His pipe smelt like sweet molasses as he told her about his travels to faraway places like Cuba, Venezuela and England.

"England, I going there soon," she said.

He enchanted her with tales of sea creatures – the angle-wing frigate birds that flew in from further north and floated on air currents; migrating whales that whistled and echoed groans to each other fathoms below; dolphins that followed ships, cavorting in leaps and twirls; and turtles that lumbered over land, but pirouetted in the sea for thousands of miles. "They track turtles now," he said. "Clip on metal tags to know where they been. I hear say that they found a turtle from here in France. And she swam back to lay her eggs, all the way home to the very same beach she born on."

He spoke of ships that passed silently in the night crewed by the ghosts of pirates and slaves thrown overboard, come back to haunt the living for generations to come. "We seamen like to believe all kind of foolishness."

Myra thought he must be over a hundred years old, but knew it was rude to ask. She wondered how his foot got to be so, like one of his mahogany roots, and imagined him carving it back into shape with a wing on the heel.

One evening, he told her about the mermaid. At night, when he was alone on deck, leaning against the rails, smoking his pipe, she would emerge from the waves, swaying to the rhythm of the sea. She waved and sang out her high-pitched promises, beguiling lonely men. But he knew better than to make the fatal mistake of looking into those eyes of hers.

"They carry 'way little children," Myra said, remembering the wailing she'd heard the night she first met him.

"Mm-hmmm. And big men too."

As the sun dipped towards the horizon behind a row of mile trees torn threadbare by the wind, he would tap his pipe against the arm of his chair – the sign that it was time for her to leave.

———

Myra knew very well that her grandmother would be horrified if she ever found out about her visits to the old man and that

punishment would be swift and severe. She and every woman of
the village had a mission to guide young girls along the right and
proper path in life. They weren't always successful. Knock-about
Patsy was evidence of that – in the rum-shop every night, boldface, holding up her glass for a refill, begging for a cigarette,
cackling like a parrot and picking fares with any man that would
take her on.

"Poor soul," Father John would say, though most thought it
was shameful – a woman's place was at home, in church and in the
store.

The Variety Store was run by Mistress Maizie, Sharkie's
reputed wife and the mother of his nine children, who provided
all essentials for survival – from lard oil, flour, Eclipse biscuits,
salt-fish and pigtail, to bay rum, Phensic, and Trumpeter cigarettes, generally bought one at a time. Honest as an angel she was,
never overcharged, and there was no weight stuck to the bottom
her scale-pan. She kept a credit book for those who had to trust,
meticulously adding what they owed, but often losing the page.
On Saturdays, she fried up a pile of her legendary fishcakes and
gave them away for free. She was "Aunty Mazie" to all the
children and gave them special treats – tamarind balls and sugar-
cakes and, sometimes, half a tin of condensed milk with nuff
spoons.

When Sharkie queried her takings, playing hard-seed, she told
him, "I doan get in you business, so best not get in mine." She well
knew he was more froth than beer. Let Peter pay for Paul was her
motto according to which she dispatched goods, balanced her
books and ensured that no one went without.

Change was slow in coming to St Lucy, a remote parish,
forsaken by the modern world, and by God, too, Father John
sometimes used to think as he went about his lifetime mission to
nurture the spiritual health and save the souls of his parishioners.
Only the women, and not all of them, accompanied by their very
young children and their very old fathers attended Sunday Wor-
ship and the grand size of the parish church made the congregation seem even smaller. After years of trying to claim the church's
proper place at the heart of village life, he compromised and

occasionally dropped in at the rum-shop to fire one – only one though, and before sunset.

"You going on one leg?" the men goaded, but they respected him as a good-good priest and appreciated his efforts with every lost sheep. That was why, they reckoned, he trekked out every Sunday after Evening Service to check on the old man and make yet another attempt to bring him back into the fold.

What they didn't know was that the two men spent their time squatting by a fire over which they roasted flying fish on a piece of wire-mesh stretched between two coral rocks. They dunked the fish into a bowl of water with salt, hot pepper and slices of onion, licked their lips, wiped their fingers – Father John on his cassock, the old man on vest that had in more holes than cloth – and discussed evolution and free will, utilitarianism and communism. Priest and outcast – two kindred souls.

One evening, it was later than usual when Myra visited. She wanted to tell him about the A she'd got for her essay, "The Lost Turtle". It was still light, but his door was shut and there was no sign of his stick. She picked her way towards the sea, the coral jooking her feet through the soles of her school shoes. She called out, but her voice was drowned by the waves, choppy with white crests against the deep blue of the water. The spray stung her face and arms. She licked the salt from her lips and curled up on his rocking chair.

The next thing she knew was his shouting. It was too dark to see his face, but his rage rang out. "What you doing here? See how late it is." He hobbled on his stick and shoved her school bag against her. As she stumbled towards the track, she heard him say, "You will get me in big trouble. Go home. Now."

Grandma Lou had dozed off as usual after the news and obituaries on Rediffusion. She woke with a start – after eight o'clock and no sign of Myra. The village, so safe by day, harboured many dangers at night, most of them imaginary, but no less scary for that. Rumours of men who came from town, grabbled up little children, especially girl-children, and carried them away under their black coats into the bush, struck fear into everyone's heart. Boys were allowed out to make sport under the street light after dark, but girls had to be safe inside and mothers had to be especially watchful. Teenage girls had been known to sneak through bedroom windows and come back with big bellies, shaming their families.

Grandma Lou threw on her shawl and her old felt hat, grabbed her cane and hustled down the road to Father John who summoned everyone to action. Sharkie's rum-shop was transformed into a rescue mission station. The men of the village, tough fishermen too-besides, strode out to search, ignoring the warnings of their women about covering up and protecting themselves against the dread afflictions of the damp night air, and moonbeams on their heads. But they were wise enough to avoid the churchyard and to watch for signs of all the duppies and devils that roamed freely at night, intent on troubling even the most devout of souls.

Myra was close to home when they found her, bedraggled and shaken, walking as if she had no idea where her feet were taking her. Her hair was like bush, school shirt hanging out at the back, shoelaces trailing behind like rat's tails. Without a word, they marched her to Grandma Lou, who spat fury, "Where you been?" She raised her hands to the heavens, grandstanding like a preacher. "Oh Gawd, look at you! Oh Gawd, look a' muh crosses!"

The women added their voices, "Answer you grandmuddah, girl. Wha' happen, cat got you tongue?"

Myra appealed to Mistress Maizie, but she turned away. And Father John had gone, he and all the men, their part done. This was women's business, the interrogation of the girl whose disappearance threatened to stain them all.

Grandma Lou stepped forward, a fierceness in her eyes, one hand on her hip, the other swinging a stinging lash across Myra's cheek. The women stuck out their bottom lips and shared thoughts on this ungrateful, fresh, force-ripe girl who had brought so much scandal and shame. Only Patsy sitting on the step outside, barefoot and wearing her usual torn dress with flowers in faded shades of blue, seemed to understand. But her hands were pressed against her lips – there was nothing she could say.

Grandma Lou began wheezing and gasping. Attention turned to her as the women put her to sit down and fanned her with an old newspaper, while Mistress Maizie poured her a shot of the sweet port wine they mixed into dark cakes. Myra stared down at her shoelaces, still undone, and chewed on a strand of her hair. She smelt her grandmother's Limacol, edged with sweat and stepped back. She covered her face with her hands and began to cry. It was what they were waiting for, and for her it was easy – she just had to make herself think about being left behind by her mother. Now they could go home.

Grandma Lou closed the front door and held out her hand. "Take off you panties."

The next day, she took Myra to the doctor, not Doctor Inniss who had treated her childhood colds and worms, put thermogene on mosquito bites and mercurochrome on coral scrapes, and once bound her sprained wrist when she fell out of a tree, but a woman in town. She wore a white tunic over a short black skirt and a stethoscope around her neck – and looked too young to be a doctor. While Grandma Lou sat upright in the waiting room, her hands clasped, eyes closed, lips moving, the doctor told Myra, "Strip down to your underwear." She sighed and shook her head as if she'd seen it all before. Under the glare of her spotlight, she examined Myra's neck and her breasts and thighs, stuck a Q-tip up inside and asked when was her last period. She gave Myra a booklet – *Adolescent Pregnancy and Motherhood* – with joyful faces of boys and girls with their beautiful babies. Soon, I going to be happy, Myra thought, just like them – because he put something in the tea that leaked through my belly-wall down into the part where babies get made. And because I sat on his rocking chair with my feet off the ground.

That was when Myra's crazy dreams started. She dreamt of baby turtles with no shells, starfish born with their tentacles knotted up, little flying fish with their fin-wings cut off, all lying belly-up on the rocks, blistering black in the sun. Out at sea, she found dolphin babies trapped in seaweed. She caught them in Grandma Lou's tea-strainer and lifted them to the surface – only one could fit at a time, but more came and more, and sharks whipping their tails against her skin like sandpaper. She floated face down. Waves rippled up over her back to her shoulders and poured into her ears, filling up her head, making it bulge like a belly-pumpkin, and burst. Myra knew that dreams carried important messages. Dreaming of dead babies must mean having a live one.

But she said nothing to her grandmother and, throughout the week that followed, she was the model good girl – home from school early, finishing all her homework and her fingernails were trim and clean. She prayed every night, "God bless Grandma and make her well again, and Mama and Father John and Aunty Maizie, and Patsy, too, keep them safe."

She didn't include the old man – she wasn't sure if to pray for forgiveness or hellfire for him and, anyway, she didn't know his name. She dabbed Limacol on her grandmother's forehead, brought her pressure pills, glasses of mauby and cups of cocoa-tea.

"Grandma, you would like Eclipse or Digestive or Shirley biscuits?"

But nothing Myra did softened Grandma Lou's heart. She only smiled in a vague kind of way, and didn't speak – not one word, not like her at all. But she prayed and prayed, and when Myra's period came, she prayed some more.

The following week, Myra could see from the way she drummed her fingers on the arm of her chair, her face set up like heavy rain coming, that she had something important to say. She pointed to the brown envelope with an English stamp on the table next to her. "You mother send for you." Inside was a plane ticket.

———

In bed that night under the cover, wearing a dark blue T-shirt and long pants, Myra was counting to stay awake. She'd reached a hundred four times when her grandmother opened the bedroom door and sat at the foot of the bed. Myra pretended to be asleep, breathing slow and shallow. She felt the pat on her shoulder and the kiss on her forehead.

She heard her grandmother, who never locked up at night, turn the keys in the front door and the kitchen door. At last, she snored in a steady rhythm. It was Myra's last chance. She eased open her bedroom window and squeezed out. Her arm caught on the latch. It hurt like a bad burn, but she covered it with the hem of her T-shirt and slipped into the shadows.

He was by the stove, pouring tea from one cup into another, as if expecting her. She lost the words she'd rehearsed in front of the bathroom mirror and stood shivering, cold bumps all over her body, biting her thumbnail like a five-year old and licking the blood off her arm. It tasted like mauby with no sugar.

He handed her a cup. "This will warm you."

Myra took a sip, but let it dribble back into the cup. "I going to England tomorrow," she blurted out. He turned away and lit his pipe. She stooped and put the cup down behind her.

"So, what happened to you hand?" he said. "Come, let this old man look at it." His claw-like fingers were as soft as feathers. The balm from a green bottle that he stroked on to her arm smelt of wood smoke. He'd never touched her before.

"That will fix it," he said. "Now child, you must go home."

I am not a child, she wanted to shout, *and my name is Myra, and I don't have a home. And I didn't tell them nothing about you. And I nearly had a baby.*

He guided her back to the track. "Walk tall, dear girl. And go well."

Myra felt so very safe, like home was supposed to be, there in the darkness, in the middle of the night, his hand on her shoulder. Yet, something was stirring inside her, a yearning, though she didn't know what for, like she was tied tight to a kite string, pulling her up and away from her childhood. England, she was going to England, at last.

———

Seven years have passed and Myra is back for Grandma Lou's funeral.

"You got to go," her mother said. "She raise you."

There has been no contact except for her duty Christmas-card-with-money-order and Myra feels no grief, no relief – no nothing. The need to have her say and put things straight has faded. But her dreams have returned – the dreams of dolphins and turtles, the mermaid beckoning, the waves closing over her head. The sight of a lame dog, even a rocking chair, brings back memories, but mostly it's the smell of ganja on a street corner, or rain on the grass in an English park – musty like the sea, calling her home.

This has to be the biggest turnout the village has ever seen. People will talk about it for years to come. The black, see-your-face-in-it hearse is the sleekest ever, the coffin has golden handles that catch the sunlight. Starched undertakers swelter in top hats and three-piece suits with tails, and dab their brows discretely with white handkerchiefs.

Myra stands with Father John inside the entrance to the St. Lucy Parish Church. He looks shrunken; his old black cassock trails on the floor.

Grandma Lou lies on white satin, wearing her bright yellow church dress and a shiny-black, straight-hair wig. Her cheeks are smoothed out so that she looks more peaceful than Myra has ever seen her. They all file in, one after the other, to pack the church full with grief and respect. Myra recognizes very few of them. They remember her though, and avoid her eyes as they lean over the coffin and hold their hands above Grandma Lou's forehead. "Bless you, may the Lord take you home safe." Together they sing her chosen hymns, chant her psalms and read her life lessons. Father John's eulogy praises her as a chosen woman of God, pillar of the Church.

"Amen," they chorus, and "Amen," again. At the graveyard, they stand together as one, and straggle through the final hymns as the coffin is lowered and earth shovelled on top, dust into dust. Grandma Lou, rock-of-ages, rest in peace.

Back at the house, Father John's faithful band of Church Army Women offers corned beef and cheese sandwiches, and the sweetbread, jam-puffs and turnovers of Myra's childhood. As she joins the men in the yard, Sharkie pulls a flask from his pocket. His voice is as loud as ever, "Just a tip," but his hand shakes as he pours a dollop of rum into her glass of coconut water. "Welcome home, Miss Myra," they say and share their memories of double-decker buses, fog thick like mud and hot water bottles. When they fall silent, she knows it's time to rejoin the women.

She sits next to Mistress Maizie, but can't remember anyone else and they don't remind her. Instead, they ask how she's managing the cold and snow. They inquire after her mother, but say nothing about how she should be here for her own mother's funeral. They avoid asking Myra when she's going back and what she's going to do with the house. But they talk about her grandmother, "a good, good woman," as if she's about to come through the kitchen door with a halo over her head and another plate of sandwiches.

Myra is struggling to chew and swallow a stodgy fishcake. Let them think what they like. I don't belong here. When will they leave? But they drone endless hymns and long, long prayers.

Mistress Maizie smiles through toothless gums; cataracts cloud her eyes. She hands Myra a white paper napkin. "Not like I used to make, eh? Is okay to spit it out. I mussee forget the baking powder. And I doan see so good now."

"How are the children?" Myra asks, remembering the story of how Maizie went to the Family Planning in town and had her tubes tied, but didn't tell Sharkie. And he said nothing about how troubled he was – not yet fifty and firing blanks.

"Big people now. Children could give plenty trouble, you know," she raises her eyebrows, "but it good to have them." She pats the back of Myra's hand, as if all is forgiven, and rejoins the hymn singing.

At last, they get to their feet, wrap the extra snacks in napkins and slip them into big black handbags. They glare at the men – time to go, this is not the North End Bar – and totter off into the night, a trail of black umbrellas up against the moonlight, winding down the road.

Father John carries empty plates into the kitchen. "She loved you, you know, the only way she knew how. You must believe that."

"I will try, Father Peacemaker, I promise." Myra takes the plates and tells him she'll clear up later. She reaches for his jacket on the peg by the kitchen door.

"Myra, wait." Father John grips her arm and pulls her to sit down beside him at the kitchen table. "He's not there. I went to see him like I did every Sunday, but he was gone." He takes a deep breath. "Gone. We searched all over, across the rocks out there. The men went out in their boats, but the sea was too rough. Nothing."

"Sea spirit," Myra whispers. "He went to her."

"What's that, my dear?"

"Nothing, Father."

He reaches down and drags a large bundle wrapped in crocus bags from under the table. "He left this on his workbench."

Before he leaves, Father John holds her hands in his. "May God bless you and keep you safe," he says, as he always has.

Inside the layers of sacking is a turtle in polished mahogany. She is a hawksbill, mounted on two metal prongs in a coral-stone base. Her eyes are open, her graceful head and limbs outstretched as if she is gliding through waves. There are no initials carved on her, and no note with her.

Myra leans forward and runs her fingers lightly over her beak and eyelids, traces the mosaic patterning on her shell. "You are home; I will never take you away from here."

She kneels, folds her arms around the turtle and lets her tears fall.

CUT GLASS

Three days of five-star tranquillity. She has given herself three days. Time enough, but not long enough to change her mind.

The bellboy, *Je m'appelle Anton Bienvenue à Martinique* on his name tag in gold letters, is busy with the remote control for the air-conditioning and another for the TV – less than half the size of her husband's latest smart, ultra-slim, curved screen.

She waves her ring-less fingers towards the glass door leading out onto the balcony. "Monsieur, er … Anton, open … s'il vous plaît. Quelquefois, les portes comme ça, er … jam, stick." She presses her hands together.

Anton nods and raises his eyebrows, as if to admire her schoolgirl French. He turns off the air conditioning, flicks a metal switch on the door, bends with the agility of a limbo dancer to remove a strip of wood fitted into the metal groove on the floor, and slides the door open. He concludes his performance with an elaborate bow.

"Voilà." His smile is radiant, carefree. "I advise that you close it, perhaps an hour before the sunset. The mosquitoes…"

I am passing for an English tourist, she thinks. *Thank you, Mom.*

She hands him a five-euro tip, not sure if it's sufficient. Her husband always dealt with money matters. But he smiles again. "Merci, mademoiselle," his voice sings, a hint of sensuality in his brown eyes, something she hardly remembers. "If there is nothing else, for now?" He closes the door behind him.

She lies on the king-size bed, arms and legs spread wide, her head heavy against the mound of soft, white pillows. Her heart has been numb for a long time, but she cannot escape the throbbing in her ribs and on the soles of her feet. She strokes her

fingertips over the dark satin bedspread and looks up at the small
spotlights embedded in the ceiling. Mademoiselle, she rolls her
tongue around each syllable.

———

His wife for two years, with nothing between them for over a
month, she took the risk. She'd rehearsed her moves, sidestepping towards him, hips gyrating, hands caressing her breasts in
the décolleté, burgundy lace camisole, her only purchase for
herself – for him. The back of his hand against her jaw pelted her
across the bedroom floor. "Whore."
 Hold your breath, hide your face. Make him go.
 His tyres screeched on the Tarmac driveway. She crawled
towards the window and closed his white velvet curtains. She
stood in the corner of his shower, on the black glinting tiles,
under cold water to dull the swelling pain, whimpering like a pet
puppy-dog left out in the rain.
 He gave her the kitten, a ball of white fluff with green eyes that
leapt in a frenzy from carpet to couch and nuzzled into her lap,
kneading with its paws, purring bliss. She laughed and clapped
her hands, overacting, "Thank you, darling. See how happy
you've made me. I will call her Maya."
 She didn't tell him it was the name she'd chosen in her poetry
days for her own baby girl, the baby girl who would never be.
 He has two faces. She never knows which one he will wear –
the pull-yourself-together and all-your-fault, or the wasn't-think-
ing and won't-happen-again. But it did, the love-beat swing –
slap, choke, burn where no one could see. And later, his sorry-
tears melting into hers, another honeymoon make up with
diamonds like chandeliers cutting into her neck, real in his world,
glass in hers.
 She has nothing left to lose. There is only the shame in her
blood.

———

She has slept all afternoon. No mosquitoes in this cool, dark
room. It's like an English countryside inn. Her mother would

love it. The colours are woodland greens and browns, the carpet and curtains plush, lampshades fringed and tasselled. She could stay hidden, safe in this darkness, but she pulls aside the curtains, switches on the light and steps out onto the balcony.

It is small. One step and she's by the bars, set waist-high in a wooden frame, only about three inches wide on top. It doesn't shake when she tests it with both hands. There is just enough space for the little table and one chair. The table has a glass top, but the chair is sturdy enough. She has chosen a room on the top floor. It looks down onto an oval swimming pool, shimmering in the artificial lights around the edges. Just a glimpse and her head spins.

She looks up at the half-moon cut into the night sky, reflecting gold. *I have become like you.*

———

She refills her glass. "So unusual to find a whole bottle of champagne in a mini-bar, n'est-ce pas?"

"Je t'en pris, cherie."

"Oh, it was you, bien sur." She giggles and empties the bottle into Anton's glass, slips back into the bath and leans against him through the overflowing pink foam with a floral scent she vaguely remembers from somewhere. He strokes her shoulders. As his hands move to her bruised ribs, she flinches and lifts them to her breasts.

"My name was Joanna," she says, "Jo, to my friends."

"Zho, I shall call you Zhosephine, la belle Zhosephine." His lips on her neck are as light as silk. She feels him harden against her lower back. *Zho, so soft and seductive.* One more time. It's been so very long. But she will not harm him.

As he slides away, she holds onto the image of his ebony back shining-wet, the dollop of froth on his shoulder.

No, not Josephine, not the Empress. Her marble statue in the town square is headless, red paint daubed over her shoulder, over the puffed sleeve and down the front of her long, white gown. The gown curves over her belly as she poses to look pregnant.

She sinks down into the water and counts to twenty-seven before surfacing. Under again, this time to thirty. She rises, choking and gasping. *So, this is what it's like.*

Her feet are cool on the tiles as she stands in front of the mirror. The muted lights flatter her slim shape. *No signs, no one would know.* She winds a towel around her dripping hair. "Don't ever cut it," he said. *I didn't – I could still go back to him.*

But she cannot go back. Instead, she plays her game, her survivor's game, one last time. She stands with her feet apart, one hand against the wall for balance, and closes her eyes. She sheds her scorched skin, peels off her branded soles, scrapes away bruises, breaks off broken bones and throws them all over her shoulder, and when there is nothing left but her face dangling in mid-air, the face he never laid a hand on after that first time, she forces herself to go one step further, to turn around, open her eyes and look at the festering red mass that once was her.

Now, she knows she can bear anything.

———

She was on the beach under a manchineal tree with her book of Maya Angelou's poems when he found her .

> *'Cause I'm a woman*
> *Phenomenally.*
> *Phenomenal woman,*
> *That's me*

"You shouldn't sit here," he said. "The leaves blister, especially your lovely skin." His long, lean face attracted her, the flickering in his eye amused her.

She was about to say, *Only when they're wet, I know, I've lived here all my life,* when he winked again. "I've been watching you."

She was only eighteen, not caring how she looked or how she spoke, carrying her mother's dreams towards a future somewhere out there, to become somebody and do something to make a difference – something brave – when he began to remodel her, this poor, pass-for-white girl.

"Your eyes change colour in the light, green to blue to grey," he said. "They are mine," he said, bewitching her, before she knew it, through the whirlwind romance, the wedding, the honeymoon in springtime Washington.

"Darling, how absolutely lovely," her new, carat-crystal voice rang out. "Do ask that man to take our photo." He indulged her then, a snapshot under pink cherry blossom, hand in hand.

"They'll be brown mush cluttering up the pavement by next week," he said, one eye blinking against the sun, stubbing out his cigarette on the cherry tree trunk, crushing it to shreds under the sole of his shoe. The signs that she denied. Like the rings he chose, the large sapphire enclosed in a circle of diamonds, the white gold wedding band binding her finger. She didn't know then that he thought he owned the air she breathed. She lost herself in this man she knew so little about.

"Children, one of each will be perfect," he said. All planned, his family plan.

―――――

She had never made big plans before, not like this. At first, it was stop-go, then it spiralled, faster than his swinging fist out of nowhere. *Fly away, fly away*, her mantra overflowed into panic.

St. Lucia? No, someone will recognise me. Martinique. Three days, it'll take him longer than that to track me down. He won't trace the money, bit by bit from his weekly house-keeping allowance. My passport, it can't be out of date. If it is, I'm stuck. Calm down, for Christ's sake.

Don't get the ticket online, he'll trace the card transaction. Pay in cash, at the airport. Get Euros there. Take a taxi, incognito. Sweet Jesus, I can't do this.

Take basics, carry-on only, my very own runaway bag. Soft-sole shoes – I'll have to walk all the way through both airports without limping – no one must remember me. Underwear, three cotton tops, nothing dressy. Take off his rings, leave them on his side of the bed for him to know. No, hide them in my bag. Flush all the pills down the toilet. Where to put the boxes? My name on the labels. Burn them, no dump them in a garbage can on the way. He will never know if I infected him. Breathe, breathe, take another pill. You can do this.

Her mother had questions: "Where to? How long? Does

he…? I could come with you."

"Oh, Mom, it's OK, really. Just taking a little break."

Fly away. No note. No loose ends.

Now, she has to be careful, to play the part. She knows how. She takes the lift down to the restaurant for breakfast, smiling, "Bonjour," and to the hotel boutique where she spends the last of her euros on a long, silk kimono, smooth and cool as coconut water. "Delightful, merci." It's irresistible – shell-pink, reminding her of herself as a child.

His colours for her were black and burgundy. "They highlight your complexion," he said.

———

She imagines bloated, yellow-grey maggots crawling through her veins, leaving sperm-slime trails after her encounter with the pick-up salsa dancer on tour, his hips like hot oil – no names, no contacts, hit and run – in his hotel room, the night before she got married.

"There is no cure. Condoms every time. And you must disclose to your husband."

"Yes, doctor." *Disclose? You have no idea.*

She paid for her last act of freedom with pills, one-a-day forever after to suppress the virus. Little yellow pills, taken on an empty stomach, taken at night so that she would sleep through the dizzy side effects, but she got the full nightmares. She hid them with all the others for sleeping and birth control, the painkillers and antidepressants, locked in the closet, behind the extra towels on the top shelf in the guest room – they never had guests – the key zipped up in her purse.

When her kitten disappeared, he shrugged. "Must have run off to get screwed, hot little bitch," the tic in his eye twitching nonstop. But she knew that even a cat could not escape his burglar bars and dead bolts. The kitten in her dreams was white as milk, strung up by the neck, green eyes slit open, pink tongue lolling. A pile of fragile bones in the palm of one hand, a skull in the other, like a broken china teacup.

It was his best yet, spinning her towards the edge. But she said nothing, played the wife to perfection, never forgetting her lines, as voices clashed in her head. His, "We belong together – I will always look after you, my love." Her own, *He'll change; today will be better, he loves me, try again, try harder. What did I do to make him so?* Her mother's, "Don't make the same mistake I did" – the trophy wife inside her respectability trap. The voice of her mother's Saviour – *Be still and know* – until she knew there was only one way out – no encore, no second chances.

————

It is early morning on her last day at the hotel. She dials the number imprinted in her memory – the number she has rung every Sunday. She will make it short: *I'm sorry. Try to understand. I love you, Mom.* She drops the phone after two rings.

Joanna walks through the glass door into the sunlight. She leans back in the chair. The sun glows red behind her eyelids, warm on her skin, like a healing balm. She could sit here and drift into gentle oblivion, but she must act – act for real this time.

She balances one bare foot on the chair, the other on the narrow wooden ledge above the bars. She hears the muffled ring of the phone in the dark room. For a moment, it seems she could go either way. But Joanna will not look down. She opens her arms. The winged sleeves of her kimono spread like pink clouds. Diamonds spark and splinter in the oval swimming pool.

MY LEFT HAND

Up to today, I don't know how I got through the funeral, especially the part when my Great Aunt B, lifted me up over the coffin for everyone to see. "Andy, kiss him, kiss him on he forehead."

Papa Joe lay there looking like someone had rubbed chalk on his face, but for all the world as if he was sleeping. I knew very well that if I touched him, he would cough and splutter, jump up and holler, "What the hell wunnuh think wunnuh doing?" right there in the big St. John Parish Church.

I struggled to get down and, for once, she did not insist. No way would she suck her teeth in the Lord's house. Those teeth were clenched, her chin up and bottom lip sticking out, and from the way she held my hand, tight but not too tight, I could tell it wasn't me she was vex with.

My mother wasn't there, she was in England. Looking back, I would have to say that Aunt B let her go to protect our family from the scandal. It was my mother who started the whole business about my two fathers.

———

Aunt B always said family business was family business. She kept herself to herself; didn't like to mix up, as she would say. Come to think of it, that could not have been easy for her, with plenty people crowding up and news spinning from one body to the next, zipping along telephone wires faster than streak lightning – this body wanting to know everything about that body and just dying to tell the next somebody. She must have had to deal with a hot nine-day talk when I was born.

But we all need someone to talk to and she trusted Miss May

– matties they were, living side by side every since. They talked through a rust-out hole in the galvanize paling, right outside my bedroom window – a jalousie window that never did shut properly. Aunt B had so many conversations out there that the ground where she stood was worn flat.

I remember her fretting one night. "And it suit she very well not to tell one of them 'bout the other one, so she could get money from all two. And the boy at school now." She was talking about my mother, about my mother having me when she was seventeen and, sorry to say, but facts are facts, not saying who my daddy was.

"Playing with fire," Aunt B hissed through the paling. "Painting she fingernails pink and she feet stuck in dirt. I tired telling she that she got to come clean, and she not listening."

Well, plenty accidents happened in those days before family planning, and there wasn't no paternity testing. Even big-shot doctors and lawyer-politicians had children that didn't look a thing like them. Everybody knew, but didn't say nothing malicious to upset things, don't mind there was lots of wizzy-wizzying about the men stepping out and the women that let them in. I like to think it was all about making sure that every one of God's children had someone to be a father to them, and love them. Whatever the case, one thing is for sure – every kitchen had a pot of family secrets on the stove, simmering safe once nobody lifted the lid.

Back then, too, there wasn't much for women to do except work as a maid for the big-ups living in town that would want you to scrub and polish all day for a piece of change that left next to nothing after you paid bus fare. Some women grew pigeon peas or maybe lettuce or thyme to sell, like Aunt B did, or kept black-belly sheep or a pig. But, mostly, the men made the little bit of money there was, and the women would stretch it and make do.

And sometimes, I have to say, they would draw up under the same men, even give them a ready-made jacket for the child support money, don't mind that didn't always work out. Like Aunt B said to Miss May one night, "Things tight and it have too many wutless men having children all about and not one red cent 'til you put them in court."

Be that as it may, my mother – well, my mother was short, with a high-brown complexion and a high-pitch voice – she used to braid hair and paint fingernails, but people thought such things should be done for free. So, what else could she do?

That's how things were. Making ends meet was an art in itself.

———

Papa Joe was my father number one – a fisherman, living up in St. John. He had a large head, a nose that catspraddled across his face and hair thick-thick and natty, reaching down his back. His hands were calloused, his fingers big like bananas. His right hand had scars from the base of his thumb across the palm from his fishing line. From since I was six, and he must have been fifty-something, Aunt B put me on the bus to spend every Saturday by him.

On evenings, we would be with his friends as they mended nets or slammed dominoes, threw back their heads and pelted down shots of rum, one-time; making sport and talking foolishness. Everybody called him "Fishbone". When I asked him why, expecting a strong-like-backbone story, he lifted me up into the air and roared, "No, no, one get stuck in my throat when I did a boy like you."

He taught me some of everything – rock fishing, flying kite, playing beach cricket with a broken oar for a bat. He cut out a thin board and sent me surfing across the sand as the waves came in. Once, he stuck his thumb in his rum and held it up for me to lick. "You's a man now." But he never took me out in his boat.

His wife said to call her, Aunty Ruby, and she never treated me like what people would call an outside child. "Hold out your hand and shut your eyes," she used to say. "Big surprise coming." And sure enough, in my outstretched hand was a sugar-cake, or tamarind ball, or a jam puff. She told me that when I was born, Papa Joe shouted – a boy, a boy at last! "I could only give him girls," she laughed.

And their house was full of girls, four of them, a rainbow of beauty and mystery. I knew nothing about girls. They loved to make joke, grabbing me and trying to kiss me, but I could duck fast enough. When I stayed overnight, I would have to watch for salt on my toothbrush, cactus in my bed, condensed milk in my shoe. I never worked out who was who, except for Alice. One day, she whispered close in my ear, "Andy, Papa can't swim. Is why he won't take you out in the boat." She was four years older than me and taller by a whole head. My golden sister – the touch of her cheek like a ripe mango, smooth and warm from the sun, has stayed with me up to this day.

We sat on the rocks, Papa Joe and me, watching whitecap waves and more waves, as if we would always be there. Like he was reading my thoughts, he gripped my shoulder and said quiet-like, "Andy, my boy, this life could turn 'round fast and kick you hard, right here." He thumped his chest.

He would take me home on the bus and, at the end of our gap, pat me on the back and give me a brown envelope. "For your Aunt B."

———

Father number two I called Father Robin when I called him anything at all. From what I heard Aunt B tell Miss May through the paling, he got so confused when he heard he was going to be a father, that he quit work as a mechanic to go lime on the block. But then he found the Lord and went to Codrington College out in St. John to train as a priest. Aunt B said he didn't have no certificates – not one! – but the college was desperate for new recruits, because all the young men were turning from the true Christian faith and going Rasta, praising Jah and smoking weed.

Thinking about it now, I figure she must have thanked God for rescuing another lost soul to pray for forgiveness for his one and only sin in life and, at the same time, shutting him away and keeping the family secret safe – at least for the time being.

Visiting was for one hour every second Friday evening. I dreaded it, walking down that long driveway with cabbage palms stretching high up into the clouds, and a dark pond on one side – you couldn't see the bottom of it.

The college loomed ahead with three enormous archways; above them three black, empty windows; and higher up, a cross – the biggest I ever saw – with Jesus hanging there looking down at me like Judgment Day come. I would walk fast, my head down, until I reached under those arches, my heart beating fit to burst.

He didn't seem short then, me being a boy and him in his long robe, but he couldn't have been more than five-foot-something. His half-glasses with silver frames sat on the tip of his pointy nose, and his mouth was small and thin. "Good afternoon, Andrew," he would say, crossing his arms and hiding his girly hands in the sleeves of his robe.

In the corner of his room was an iron bed with a coconut husk mattress, a folded brown blanket and a thin pillow. Above it hung a small wooden cross. On the concrete floor was a mat with a hole in the middle and a grey lump of coral-stone to keep the door open. On the wall, a notice board with his timetable for lessons in Old Testament Christian Ethics and such like, and a clock with thin black hands like sea-urchin spikes.

The only brightness in that room was the sunbeam across his desk where he had me sit and draw – a chicken feather, a dried-up mango seed, a snail shell, a mahogany pod split open so you could see the seeds packed tight and tidy. He paced the floor, hands clasped behind his back and leant over my shoulder. "Texture, perspective, shape, shade," he said, blinking slow like a lizard. "Good enough, but you must pay more attention to detail."

He looked at me like he couldn't understand where I'd come from, but he didn't move the pencil from my left hand like they did at school with lashes from a ruler across my knuckles. When I caught his eye, looking hard at my hand, he turned his head, quick so, and I would peek at the clock hands flicking from quarter to five to five to, and time up. He gave me the still life to practice when I got home, but I always pelted it through the bus window.

The envelopes he gave me were small and white. He wrote my mother's name on them with his left hand. Aunt B snorted when she opened them. "Don't you tell him you mother gone 'way."

When I asked why, she snapped, "You too gypsy. Why you must know everything?"

————

My Aunt B called herself poor, peaceful and polite, and mostly she was – peaceful that is – especially after my mother left. She and me and her big orange cat – Puss, she called him – to me he was Tiger – lived together loving for the most part. But you couldn't fool her, not one bit. And she had a tongue sharper than Aunty Ruby's knife for boning fish. Like when she trimmed my hair: "Siddown and hold still, or a piece of you ear going get cut off", or my fingernails, "You going be one finger short."

She would take down the strap from the hook by the kitchen door to share lashes across my back, my legs – whatever part she could reach. That is how it was for children in those days. Tenderness was against the rules for raising children, especially boys, who had to be made tough for life. So they would catch you tail afire, licks like peas, to beat out the deceitfulness and the lying, *for the truth will set you free*; beat out the bad blood and wickedness, beat out the spoilt child and the poor great, *for you must know your place in life;* beat in manners and broughtupcy; beat in ABC and two-four-six. And beat in the love.

"Hard-ears wouldn't hear, hard-ears you going feel". And then a tongue-lashing – like all the crosses she had to bear were burning up inside her. Lord have mercy. She chasing, me running, the cat screeling – out into the yard, around her kitchen garden, behind the breadfruit tree, and back inside to the only places of safety – under her bed. The cat would be on top of her closet arching its back. She would kneel down and swat the strap forward and back, but it never reached me flat against the wall, holding my breath, waiting for her huffing to slow down, for the mattress to sag as she sat on it, and her deep chuckle, telling me it was safe to come out and the cat to come down. Not that her tongue was done. "Next time, I goin' cut you tail, good and proper."

When I was five and ready for elementary school, Aunt B instructed, "Never say nothing 'bout either one of them." But all the boys boasted about their fathers. If you didn't have one to brag about because he was dead or gone to America or lock up in Glendairy Prison, you felt left out. So, I boasted about Papa Joe and his locks like a lion, and the time he caught a shark six-foot long. I never said nothing about Father Robin, and that was no problem since he was well out of sight anyway.

Up to then, I mostly featured my mother. My face, looking back at me from the bathroom mirror, told me nothing. I would put a little water in a glass and toss it down my throat, pull up my T-shirt and puff out my chest. I held up my right hand, small, but not that small. And I measured my height on the wall with a ruler, willing the mark to go up. All us boys did that.

Mostly, life moved on, easy so. But I remember one set of confusion when Father Robin was finally ready to leave the college to be a parish priest, and the parish happened to be St. John. When I asked Aunt B if I had to visit him there, she got hot. "Yes, and why you like to ask so much questions?"

What a to-do-ment! Blue vex she was, but she calmed down and it was back to Father Robin on a Friday evening, Papa Joe on Saturday, church with Aunt B on Sunday, and school on Monday morning.

———

But you never know what coming in life. You could be up today, back down tomorrow, and the down coming when you not looking, just when you feeling cool and good. One Saturday, Alice met me at the bus stop. "Papa in the hospital. Sugar-foot, they had to cut off two of he toes."

He had diabetes. I think it was more than that, but nobody told me nothing. Those days, they didn't used to tell children about real serious things like malnutrition and abortions and obeah and homosexuality – and the Big-C, as they called it. They would just speak low without moving their lips, or send you out to sweep the yard and pick caterpillars off the lettuces.

Aunty Ruby cussed him out, "You's a foolish hardback, old man that feel you could carry on as you like and live forever." Because that's just what Papa Joe was doing when he came home, liming and drinking the same way, and bawling blue murder at the nurses when they came to change his dressings.

"Stop humbugging me, woman," he said. It was back to the hospital a year later.

"Andy, them have to cut off he foot now, up to here," Alice said, slicing under her knee with the edge of her hand, then lifting the hem of her T-shirt to wipe her tears and hide her face. I didn't know what to say. She hugged me, smelling like vanilla ice cream, and gave me a little silver coin. "For luck, hold it tight-tight, and pray for Papa."

It was like the spirit got punched out of him. He hobbled with a wooden crutch, his useless half-leg dangling. He shaved off his locks. His head looked like a football with the air sucked out, his ears big, as if they were growing. Even his laugh dried up, like the rest of him. He sold his boat and nobody called him Fishbone no more.

"Son, life is a funny thing." He stared over my shoulder. "You got to take every day as it come." That was the last thing he said to me. I was only eight.

———

Like the whole parish had to be there that afternoon, don't mind the heavy rain. People that came late stood outside under big black umbrellas. The fishermen, in the rumpled suits they must have had since their own children's christenings, nodded weather-beaten faces. "You a'right, Andy boy?"

I was hot and sweaty in a borrowed suit, too small and pinching under my arms. The grief lump in my throat wouldn't swallow, and not just because Aunt B pulled the tie I was wearing too tight. My belly was growling. Earlier, she had fixed my favourite fried chicken and macaroni pie and plantain, but I could only push it around the plate.

Father Robin – everybody called him that now – was standing at the entrance in his robes with Papa Joe's girls, all in black. Alice and Aunty Ruby were sitting to one side and didn't see us arrive, or when Aunt B lifted me up with her "kiss him, kiss him" talk.

As Father Robin began, "Dearly Beloved...," I fell asleep. Now I know that Aunt B let me sleep – didn't jook her elbow in my side like she usually did at church to keep me from nodding off – so I would miss the eulogy about Papa Joe being the father of four beautiful girls, and how he wanted a son and, having a generous Christian spirit, he adopted me. I only heard about that years later.

In the church yard, the coffin wobbled as the men staggered in the mud to hold the ropes tight and lower it into the grave. Standing behind Aunt B, my head buried in her back, her hand on my shoulder, I heard the grave diggers' spades *chunk, chunk, chunk* into the earth, like they would never stop, trying not to think of him all alone down there in the darkness, pressing Alice's coin in my pocket so hard it left a print on my thumb.

"The day Thou gavest, Lord, is ended. The darkness falls..." I wanted to run, the two of us, me on his back holding his locks, across the cane-fields, to the sea, to sit on the rocks and watch the waves.

"For ever and ever..."

But his locks were gone. And I felt like a crab in a hole.

"...Amen. Come, that's enough." Aunt B tugged my hand and we went to sit on a bench by the church, away from the sobbing and lamentation. I scraped mud off her shoes with a stick and she patted my head, as if she was going to say something but, instead, opened her bag and handed me a pack of Shirley biscuits. We stared through the flickering leaves of the mahogany trees. The sun went down and darkness fell.

It was one of those fresh nights with no clouds when sounds travel clear and sharp. "The turnout was real big, don't mind they had us sitting at the back," Aunt B told Miss May with a sniff, her voice louder than usual. "And Andy behave good, standing strong like a man for he father."

Plenty time had to pass for me to understand she wanted me to hear every word, bless her. Maybe, too, she wanted me to kiss him, to show the whole congregation that I was somebody to him – she who always said that you must know your place.

———

The next person to die was Aunty Ruby, less than two years later. I had been back there only once, but that Christmas, I had the great idea of baking a ham to take for them. Aunt B was making me cook. "You don't have no sisters to do for you. You got to be independent." So mostly it was to show off my new skills to Aunty Ruby and Alice. But Aunt B said, "I hear them not doing so good now. Just take some dark cake. And you could make some coconut bread."

Alice opened the door. She took the package I'd brought and pointed to a chair at the table. "You could sit there." I barely recognized Aunty Ruby, like a shadow in a black dress with buttons down the front. She gave me a glass of mauby and asked about school and Aunt B's health. The girls, all four of them, sat around the room watching me from every angle. Alice left the room. I wanted follow her, but dared not move.

She came back carrying Papa Joe's fishing rod. "He left this for you. He said to tell you so you could always eat, whatever happen in life."

Aunty Ruby held out half a pumpkin in a plastic bag. "For your Aunt B".

"Is OK. You keep it," I said. "Aunt B got plenty pumpkin in her kitchen garden."

"You still very young, Andy," Aunty Ruby said as she touched my forehead. She laid the pumpkin on the table and went into the kitchen. Behind the closed door, pots and enamel bowls clanged and clattered.

"You too ungrateful," one of the girls hissed. "And selfish," said another, "just like you mother." I jumped up, but Alice got between us and pushed me through the front door. My package lay unopened on the table.

At the bus stop, Alice handed me the pumpkin. "It's not for you," she said, "and not your place to say, no." She stood in silence, looking everywhere but at me. I was glad enough when the bus came. As it turned the corner, I looked back at her standing there, holding on to the bus pole.

I didn't go to that funeral, didn't want to see any of them ever again. Aunt B went. "Like Ruby couldn't live without him," she told Miss May.

———

Then it was Aunt B. It seemed like normal old age creeping on. I rubbed her knees with Bengies and fixed ginger tea for her pains from the gas working under her arm, a little white rum for the bad feels. But it got worse – her clothes obzokey, skirt on inside-out, hair tangled up and a foul smell on her breath. I found our toothbrushes stuck upright in the garden next to her dried-up lettuces. "Wicked spirit put them there," she said. I didn't understand what was happening. I had thought, as children do, that she would last forever.

Lying in my bed at night, I heard her wailing, "Sweet Jesus, have mercy, so much things vexing my spirit." After that came the muttering. I held her hands. "Aunt B, what day it is today? What is the queen's name?" Her eyes were vacant and her lips moved, but she couldn't find the words. Later, I found her on the ground in the yard, her nightdress soaked, one slipper on the wrong foot. She reached to stroke my cheek, her hand trembling like a candle flame. "Archie, Archie, my sweet love." I fled next door to Miss May. We wrapped her in a towel and took her inside. All I could feel was bones. "Elizabeth," she beamed. "She name Elizabeth. The Second." I couldn't bear it.

When my mother phoned, I asked her about Archie.

"How you hear 'bout him?"

"Aunt B."

"What she said?"

"Nothing, just the name. Who he is?"

"Never you mind. Lemme speak to she."

"She in the bathroom," I lied.

"Go get her. I waiting."

My mother arrived with her bribes: a Timex watch, Marks & Spencer's long pants, Quality Street chocolates. She dumped Aunt B in an old folks' home and scurried around like a crazy fowl, selling everything she could – furniture, curtains, pots and plates – shoving the rest into big black plastic bags for the garbage men to collect. She had a real estate agent come to value the property, padlocked the windows and doors, and left an extra set of keys and the cat with Miss May.

On the plane to England, as she slept with a smile on her lips, I tried to remember when she was my mummy, my own queen. Once, when a boy at school said she was too fast, I got mad as hell and cuffed him.

I stuck my fingers into the seat belt buckle and squeezed. If only I had read the Bible to Aunt B instead of asking stupid questions, her mind would have come back. If I had come home early from school to feed her and brush her teeth… I mashed the buckle again and again. If I had kept my big mouth shut on the phone, we would have got through. If I loved her more like she loved me… I pounded down, until my finger nails were black and bleeding, feeling nothing.

I stayed with my mother and her English husband and their two daughters for six long years. "You got to be nice. He is you step-daddy," she said.

I could have challenged her then. I wonder if she even knew which one was my father, but it no longer mattered. And, for sure, I didn't need another one.

"And he paying for you aunt to stay in a good home," she said. But Aunt B already had a good home. And Aunt B and Aunty Ruby were my mothers, and Alice my special sister – all of them more real.

When I was eighteen, I got a scholarship and escaped to art college in London. Papa Joe and Aunty Ruby had faded from my thoughts – Alice, too. Even Aunt B – I'd convinced myself that there was no point keeping in contact since she no longer knew who I was. The self-centredness of youth, looking forward not back, there were days when I didn't think about any of them at all.

Then a lawyer wrote to say that Aunt B had died. She'd left her home to me.

It had never sold and, by the time I returned, sixty-five and retired, there was nothing left but a piece of galvanise paling full of rustholes, a kitchen garden overrun by love vine. Under a pile of rubble, I found Papa Joe's fishing rod, broken in half.

I got it all cleared away and built this wall house with a gallery at the back, overlooking Miss May's empty old house. I'm here now with my thoughts and a glass of rum and coconut water, at that quiet time when the day sighs and closes into night. The birds pause their twittering and the wood-doves their mournful cooing, as if they're waiting for the tree frogs to chirrup their call and answer, and the fireflies to flicker and come alive. The noise of traffic fades; even the staked-out kites seem to respect this moment of stillness. The leaves of Aunt B's breadfruit tree turn and settle down, bowing as the moon lifts her full belly over the horizon and slides behind the clouds to give the stars their turn. The cat slinks in, stretches and rubs against my legs, as if it's adopted me. It's white with brown patches, not orange, but I like to think it's family to Tiger-Puss, come back home, like me.

I paint, mostly landscapes of the sea with rocks and fishing boats, his voice still guiding me. *"Texture, perspective, shape, shade."* When my fingers are too stiff, it's greeting cards. *"Attention to detail…"* Poinsettia and snow on the mountain for Christmas and scarlet Valentine hearts. I can hear Aunt B suck her teeth, loud and long. No bright and easy love-hearts for her, she who never spoke about love until she no longer knew what she was saying.

Occasional commissions come my way. One was to paint Codrington College. I could have done it from memory, but went back with my fold-up easel and stool. The door of Father Robin's room was locked. I walked around the building and looked through the window. Inside was dark, but for a moment, I was sure I saw a robed shadow pacing the empty room, hands clasped behind his back. I felt his breath on my neck, so real that I spun around into the sun.

And Alice? Dear Alice, she's been living alone in the same house since Aunty Ruby died and her sisters went to America. I take the bus there on Saturdays, as I used to all those years ago. We do domestic things – I change light bulbs and sweep the yard while she cooks. We eat, talk of this and that, and doze off in separate armchairs. What might have been between us – Alice and me – hangs in the air, trapped in a bubble with a skin too thick to burst.

Maybe though, maybe one day, we will be free to share what Aunt B and Aunty Ruby knew from the start, but hid to protect me; what Papa Joe must have known but figured didn't matter; what Father Robin knew but couldn't take on – the truth there in my left hand every time I pick up a paintbrush.

Like Aunt B always said, the truth will set you free. But

sometimes it must wait until you grow to be an old man. Up to then, the love going round and coming round will keep you safe. The love in a silver coin and a jam puff, in a lick of rum and a fishing rod, even in a dried-up mango seed or packed tight in a mahogany pod. And all the love wrap-up in a mini-pack of Shirley biscuits, holding your truth until you ready for it.

REFLECTION

He phones, "Hi, I heard you were back." He pauses. "Be good to see you." He's choosing his words, trying to keep it light.

See me, after all these years? Twenty-seven, to be exact. What's the point? "Well, yes, but I've got so much... only here for four days."

He persists – not like him at all. "Same place?"

The place is not the same. It's now The Scarlet Lounge with bright red walls and yellow lights dangling from silver stems. Glitzy black tables and chairs with chrome legs have replaced the old wooden ones with patched denim cushions. Warhol prints of Jackie with luscious, red lips and Marilyn on blue with blue eye-shadow hang on one side of the room. The other is mirrored from floor to ceiling, a clever device, but the ceiling is low and the room claustrophobic and full of young people. They prattle and brag above the cacophony of plates and glasses, and the espresso coffee machine. Definitely not his kind of place, not anymore.

There he is, in the far corner, his back to me. His profile, reflected in the mirror, looks much the same, but he's shaved off all his hair. Not a fashion statement, surely. Not him. Still has that coarse little moustache – grey now, though. And nobody wears shirt-jacs these days. White or off-white? Difficult to tell in this light. Hasn't put on weight, no potbelly, got to admire that. He's staring at the floor, eyes half closed.

"Welcome, Miss. Table for one?"

"Er, no. I'm meeting..." I point. The waiter raises his eyebrows.

"Hello, James." Always James, never Jamie, Jimmy or Jay.

He blinks. "Ah, Katie." I've been Katherine since I left, but I let it pass. He stands; we hug and sit opposite each other. "You look great; you've cut your hair."

"You, too." We laugh. It's awkward, not like we used to laugh. "And how's the family?" One kid or two? I don't remember.

"The children – young people, I should say," he grins, "are fine. I think." I have to lean forward to hear him.

"You think?"

"Well, they're abroad. Coming home soon, though." He gives me the facts about the two of them. He never talked emotions. I give up struggling to listen through the noise. And do I really want to know? My fault for asking. I try to look interested, but I'm checking his appearance and body-language. It's instinctive and I'm good at it – my interrogation skills as an investigative reporter. The top button of his shirt is missing and his fingernails are ragged. But he gives nothing else away, never did.

We feisty feminist students used to compare notes after our dates. Describe him using only two words. Mine for James were *tight* and *uptight*. Still, we were together for over two years. Whatever did I see in him?

Shabby, that's the word for him now. Only 49, same age as me. If that's what marriage and children do to you, thank goodness I stayed clear.

"You're miles away," he says. "What'll you have?"

"What?"

"To eat. Smoked salmon salad, like last time?"

Like last time? He remembers from so long ago? I should go, now. "No, I'm…"

"Would you like to go somewhere else?" He puts his hands over his ears. There is a dullness in his eyes. Must be a reflection of the light.

"No, no, this is fine."

"This place…" He looks bemused, as if he expected it to be the same.

"Are you having anything?"

"Just water. But you should. You need the energy. Lots to do, people to see." That smirk of his is still there.

"Water for me, too. Actually, I do have a meeting, at two-thirty."

"Busy lady." Another smirk. I really have to get out of here. But why the hell did he want to meet? He waves for the waiter who takes no notice.

"Still teaching?" I ask.

"No, no, early retirement."

"And Shirley?"

"OK, she's coping…" He looks around, pulls the front of his shirt together and goes to get the waiter.

Shirley Belle, law student, the year below us, trapping James with her sharp fingernails, her cute ass and her pregnancy. The wedding, immediately after graduation, was held on the clipped lawn of her parents' home in Jamaica – Cherry Gardens. Big white marquee, seats covered in white tied with bows, a bamboo arch threaded with white roses, below which they stood, the bride in white, if you please, her lace sleeve wedged under his arm. Decent, do-the-right-thing James – he avoided me the whole evening. Well, I was wearing a long black crepe skirt cut on the bias, and an outrageous, crimson silk camisole. What did I care? Had another life planned. Trainee BBC reporter. Jet-setting. Independent.

James returns, the waiter following. "Just two waters, please – bottled, not tap." Up go the waiter's eyebrows again.

My turn to lighten things up. "You and bottled water?"

He used to rant on, "Absolutely nothing wrong with tap." *Tight.*

"Don't smoke," he says as I pull cigarettes from my bag. I ignore him, of course. *Uptight.* "Please." I replace the pack.

"So, Katie, how have you been?"

I'll keep it short. "Oh you know, Geneva, Paris…"

"And the new apartment?"

How did he know? "Oh, it's great. Islington's great. Lovely cafés…" He's got me gushing and him cool and thoughtful – that hasn't changed.

"You are still so beautiful."

"…view over the park. What?" My mouth hangs open.

"Beautiful, you."

He pulls a beige envelope from his shirt pocket. His hand

trembles. "I should have given you this. Ever since… Or thrown it away." He shrugs and slides the envelope across the table towards me. "Back in a minute." He shuffles between the crowded tables to the gents, holding on to the backs of chairs.

Inside the envelope is a small box, inscribed *Janelle's Jewellery,* inside that a pendant, made with beach glass, a piece from a blue bottle worn smooth by the sea. It is the size of a dollar coin and encircled by a fine thread of silver wire wound into a small loop. It's exactly what I'd have loved, then.

———

On our stolen weekends at the East Coast we collected beach glass in brown, white and green – blue was rare. We walked all the way to Round Rock and back in each other's footprints – me striding, you tiptoeing, both laughing. We had the whole beach to ourselves, us and your stray puppy – black it was, with one eye – you chasing as it scampered to catch crabs, you on all fours imitating, rolling over, sand in your golden hair and moustache. Round Rock, big as a house. "Let's climb to the top," I said. "No way," you said, grabbing my foot. Holding me safe or holding me back? Until I broke free.

I remember the waves pounding, the sun on my back, your towel over my head, as we sheltered from the pelting rain, your arm around my shoulders, your amber eyes glowing desire, the only time I ever saw you push the puppy away.

He must have hidden it from me, this blue gem, had it specially made up, kept it all these years. I hold it against my throat and look at myself in the mirror. I should have kept my hair long, worn a cotton dress in matching blue, like the one Katie used to wear.

———

He makes his way back to the table. No hair, pallid eyes, trembling hand. Bottled water, "Don't smoke". Shit. Early retirement, Shirley coping, children coming home. So many signs. How could I be so blind?

"Thank you. I love it." I mouth the words and reach to hold his hand. As he leans over and kisses my forehead, I see his ribs and smell his sallow staleness. His head reflects the yellow light. I want to stroke it.

He looks at me. "Katie, I've always…" The rest is lost in the clatter of plates.

"What? Say that again. Let's go somewhere quiet." I take out my smartphone. "I'll cancel the meeting."

"No, don't do that. Off you run. It must be important." He winks. He knows there's no meeting, sees right through me. Always did. The waiter brings two plastic bottles of water and glasses. "Have mine," he says and pulls his hand away. He pays and leaves.

I swallow a mouthful of the water. It's after two-thirty and everyone's left. The waiter hovers in the doorway.

I hate him, hate his "busy lady", his "off you run." I gulp the water. I hate him for leaving me alone, for taking his kind of loving, his "still so beautiful." I start on the second bottle.

The Scarlet Lounge is silent. There's no one to hear as I crumple his empty bottle in my fist. Damn him and his dollar-bit of broken glass.

I turn to the mirror. Make-up's a mess. I like my hair short, though. Grey roots showing, but soon fix that with a comb. I'll just slip into the ladies.

I wonder how long he's got.

FAMILY HOME

"That woman," Merlese sputtered as she thumped her gold bag on the kitchen table. "That woman – like she got Pa bewitch. You see how she playing she going fall? In the Lord's house, tuh besides." She slumped onto one of the four matching chairs and squeezed off her white, too-tight shoes.

"Mer, hush, nuh." Rosine put on the kettle and reached up to the shelf where she kept her teas. *Calming chamomile with fevergrass.* She put a teaspoonful into the mug with the big pink M on it. "Her name is Gloria…"

"How you know that?" Merlese snorted.

"…Gloria Gooding, come back from New York."

"Gloria my ass. She name Jezebel. And she doan belong here no more. See she parading she bony self in that fancy yellow suit from over 'n away, she waist tight like vice?" Merlese pursed her lips. "Communion, and she like she at the Governor General tea party."

Rosine sat down opposite Merlese, lifted her skirt and pulled her sister's foot onto her lap. She massaged the bloated ankle with smooth strokes, her hands cool and firm. She watched Merlese's eyes droop and her mouth hang open.

Rosine thought she took after Papa. A home-bird, she kept herself to herself; didn't care much about life out there. Merlese was like Mama, always out and about – mixing up with all kinds of people, and plenty men too. At twenty-nine, Rosine was two years younger, but she was careful about what she said and often felt it was best to keep her thoughts to herself. Sometimes she felt like the calm eye of the storm while Merlese clamoured around her.

"That woman have Pa tie up with she dirty tricks. The two of them up in their seventies. Cuh dear, them doan got no shame? Rose, you cahn see what going on?"

And your hot mouth has no cover. But Merlese was only giving voice to Rosine's own fears. Troubling her day and night was the image of Papa rushing across the aisle to that woman as she stumbled. He held her arm in his, close to his heart for the whole congregation to see, and guided her out of the church and down the road towards her house across the gully, not once looking back.

———

Their family home started as a modest wood house – two-roof with a shed-roof perched on a groundsel of coral-rocks – one of a row along the road that ran through the village. Each had enough space for a small front garden and a backyard, separated from the neighbours' with galvanise paling. Over the years, board and shingle had been replaced by wood, then concrete. Rosine liked that the neighbourhood had grown more private and peaceful. Now you scarcely heard the hollering of unmannerly children, out-of-hand women getting licks, the raucous rum talk, and the disgusting carry-on of sex that escaped through the cracks in wooden walls. Homes were more stylish. Jalousies had given way to glass windows with blinds; old-time hip-roofs to flat ones, though Papa said that high winds could lift them up and carry them away, easy so. Locks and burglar bars appeared on doors and windows, fences and hedges went up, and front gardens had colour-coordinated flower beds, don't mind some went too far with their show-off features from America – bird baths and fairy lights and yellow sunshine ornaments.

Here was where Papa and his sister and brother were born and raised. Aunt Ada had left to train and work as a nurse in London. Uncle Morty was a seaman and could never settle down any place. Just now, he lived across the pasture with some woman and her five children – the last two little ones were supposed to be his. So that left Papa at home and, when they got married, Mama moved in. After the girls grew up, Merlese went to live in town and Rosine stayed home, though she worked every day at the local primary school, where she sorted and re-shelved library books and generally helped out, so there wasn't much company for Mama and she was real restless. When her father, died and the money came to her, she set about building herself a dream house – a bungalow.

The walls went up block by block around the old wood house. All the dust and botheration made Papa cough a lot, but he didn't complain. The front-house became the "living room," according to Mama, repainted in marigold yellow. "Like livin' in a egg yolk," Papa said. Out went the china cabinet, the linoleum and Papa's worn-out, brown armchair with pockets at the sides for his newspapers. In came the three-piece suite, the coffee table and the drapes with palm-leaf motif. The guest room was added – "en suite", if you please. The old kitchen was stripped and workmen from Luxury-Style-Homes Inc. invaded with their hammering and drilling and their rude-boy jokes. Mama had started on her "master bedroom" with matching curtains and bedspreads in lavender with fine magenta stripes – two bedspreads because, as Rosine overheard her say to Papa, two single beds were "more decent" at their time in life.

Papa rescued his armchair and retreated to the shed in the yard. He was out there for hours with wutless Uncle Morty who snuck in through the back gate with his flasks of rum. Rosine couldn't understand how they got on so well, being so different – but blood is blood. She'd stand at the kitchen sink by the open window, scrubbing sweet potatoes or scaling fish while they sipped their Old Gold with plenty joke and old-talk about how the new minister of drains and gutters made a pappyshow of fixing the bridge across the gully. "Politricks." Sometimes they lowered their voices so she couldn't hear.

One evening, Papa held his hand in front of his mouth and whispered, "Rosie, guess what? The money run out. Restoration done; deliverance come." They shared one of their special looks.

Frustration at having her interior decoration project cut short sent Mama's blood pressure way up. The first stroke put her in bed; the second, well, that was the end, despite Rosine running up and down from kitchen to bedroom to bathroom with bowls of water, bottles of Limacol, glasses of lemonade with bitters, and cans of floral spray to take away the dull yellow smell of stale sweat and bad breath.

There was the day she called from the kitchen, "Mama, you want green tea, cocoa tea or bush tea?"

There was no answer.

———

Merlese came home, but it was Rosine who got Papa through it all. One set of phone calls and neighbours traipsing in with their condolences, the funeral service with plenty hymns, readings and psalms – already chosen by Mama. And Merlese bawling the place down. After she'd gone back to town, Rosine and Papa slipped into an easy routine. At twenty past eight on mornings, she left for work, but was home every evening to take care of him. She knew his needs and desires. He especially liked steamed flying fish with rice and peas and her homemade seasoning. On Saturday mornings, he loaded the washing machine and hung out the clothes; she pressed and folded them. She mopped and dusted, and trimmed the plants in the front garden, while he cleaned up the yard and pottered about in the shed. On Sundays, they went to church together. In her shoes with their stacked two-inch heels, Rosine was the same height as Papa, walking in step, side by side.

The kitchen was where they spent time together. They brought back in Papa's armchair and moved the Formica table to make space for it. Like a faithful old donkey, sagging in the middle. Rosine patched the holes in the arms where the stuffing was coming out. She moved the television in from Mama's living room, but left the wedding photo, which had been on top of it. As a child, she used to look at it with her right eye shut and her head tilted to the left to cut her mother out of the picture.

At seven o'clock, Papa would watch the news. Later, he'd read to her from the *Daily Nation* as she washed the wares, though she only half listened to the goings-on in the outside world. Much of the time, the only sounds were the humming of the fridge and the clock ticking. They knew each other so well, there was no need to say out loud what they were thinking.

But since that thing happen at church, with the woman pretending to fall, Papa was hardly ever home. And, when he was, it was as if she wasn't there. She felt she couldn't ask, but she had to know. So, one Saturday morning, when he'd gone down by Uncle Morty, or so he said, she searched.

In his bedroom, in the shoebox in the closet, she found the letter. The envelope had a US stamp and was addressed to Mr. Mortimer Clarke. Inside was another envelope marked *CONFIDENTIAL* with her father's name on it. The letter, in bold italic handwriting, said how life might have been different if she had never left, how she was *unwell*, and *planning to come home*. It ended with *affection from your childhood friend, Gloria Gooding*. It was dated the month before Mama died.

It meant nothing – just a letter between childhood friends. But why was it sent to Uncle Morty? And why had Papa hidden it, and never said a word about her?

She folded the letter and replaced it in one deceitful envelope, then the other. *My own Papa, how could he?*

She would wait for him to come to his senses. She watched as he drank the tea she made for him, but hardly ate anything, no matter how she tried to tempt him with his favourites.

"How you have in here so hot?" he said one evening. He struggled out of his armchair and shuffled to the window to open it. The sight of this sorry old man made her feel bold.

"Papa," she said, "I could ask you a question?"

"Mmmm?"

"The lady at church, she OK?"

"No."

"She going back to New York?"

"No. She can't." His eyes met hers for a second before he turned his back and looked out through the window.

"Goodnight, Papa." Rosine went into her bedroom and shut the door. Now he will have to stop this foolishness. He will hate for me to know he's carrying on, just like his two-timing brother.

———

One evening, Papa came home early. He held her shoulders and kissed her cheek. They ate together at the kitchen table and he finished every last mouthful of the chicken with yam pie and fried plantain.

Rosine allowed herself to think everything was back to normal.

He read her horoscope: "The journey you have been waiting for." He folded the newspaper and patted the arm of his chair. She perched beside him. "Rosie, is no life for you here. That counselling you wanted to train for, you would be good at it. You should go. Go to London."

"But Papa, you and me…"

He raised a warning hand. "You could meet a nice young man."

Rosine stood.

"I speak to Aunt Ada already."

Rosine walked across the kitchen and began to wash the wares.

"She have a spare room that she making special for you."

Rosine gripped the edge of the sink.

"And I book the flight for you to go, next month."

She heard his retreating footsteps and the door shut behind him. She grabbed the newspaper with wet hands and tore open the pages. There was no mention of a journey. He's getting rid of me. He has it all planned.

———

Ever since she was a teenager, Rosine had known that she, not Merlese, would stay home and look after Papa and Mama in old age. She was content. This was where she belonged. She was the light of loving care in their home.

When Merlese came back on weekends, she slept in the guest room. It had its own bathroom, after all. They moved her bed out of the room they had shared as children. It was Rosine's now. Merlese always caught the four o'clock bus back to town on Sundays. Good thing, too, the way she filled the house with her voice bellowing through every room, stomping and rattling the glassware. She bombarded Papa with nonstop speechifying about the cost of living and the young people of today, and public affairs that no longer concerned him. When Rosine told her not to tire him out, she yelled, "He's my father, too."

And Merlese never put things back where they belonged. After she left, Rosine calmed herself by humming her favourite hymns as she sorted plates according to size and forks that got mixed in with spoons, and moved butter and cheese to the compartment in the door of the fridge and tomatoes to the tray below.

"Tidy-up time again?" Papa would smile.

But Merlese was entitled; it was her home, too. Even men like Uncle Morty, who travelled far away and had women all about – even he had the right to return to where he was born and raised, and bring his children and his children's children. Imagine the confusion if that happened, Rosine thought. But there was no way Merlese would come back – too dull for her. Uncle Morty hadn't put one foot inside after the marriage; didn't get past the shed. Mama had never even called his name. He was "the vagabond that doan know how to keep he tail quiet." He belonged down the road with his own outside family.

Everything had been the way it should be. Until Madam Gloria Gooding turned up from New York. Now Papa was telling her to leave, his favourite daughter, his only sweet girl. He had no right. It was all wrong.

———

Early one Sunday morning, Rosine sat at the kitchen table sipping a cup of lemon balm tea, her diary open in front of her. She had tried to make sense of everything by writing it down, but that only made it more real. She crossed out her notes, tearing the page with her pen. The "go, go, go" of his voice troubled her like nothing ever had.

She heard Merlese stirring in the guest room. *She will cuss and carry on, but soon stop. Rejection – that's how people will see it but soon forget me, alone and cold in a London spare room.* Rosine choked back her tears.

She leant over his empty armchair. "Alright then," she hissed, "I will go. I've had enough of all the cooking and cleaning and tidying up. And you so ungrateful. See how you going get through without me."

Rosine gulped the last of her tea. *That wicked woman, how could he let her turn his mind?* She imagined him walking to church with her, dancing close, his arm around her waist. She saw her making style in Mama's fancy living room; saw him holding her hands across the kitchen table, looking into each other's eyes; saw them....

Merlese burst in. "Pa didn't come home last night. His bed, he didn't sleep in it." She stood in the doorway, holding up her finger. "Rose, listen good; I had enough of this shite. I going down there and find out what going on."

Rosine snapped her diary shut. "No. No, you can't do that."

"And why not, pray tell?"

"It's none of your business," Rosine said. "And he would tell you to go, too."

"What?"

"Nothing. Leave me alone."

"Alright, I going," Merlese said. She caught the morning bus back to town.

———

Rosine could be real stubborn. "Own-way," Papa said with a wink, but she got it from him. He used to tell the girls that, once he'd made up his mind, not even a force five hurricane could change it. She waited until after midnight, put on her lace-up shoes, wrapped a black shawl over her dark green dress, and crept into the night. There was no moon, but she kept to the shadows, away from the streetlights. She was thankful that it was drizzling. The umbrella would hide her face. Careful not to slip on the mud, she walked across the pasture and over the bridge. She knew the way well. This was not the first time she had followed her father.

The house – no more than a hut – was set back from the road, in darkness under the massive, spreading branches of a breadfruit tree. It was unpainted with a galvanise roof eaten out by rust. *How some people could dress down in their glad rags, but can't bother to fix up their home?*

Rosine stepped through the damp, long grass to avoid the crunch of gravel on the path, and between the clay pots of tangled, dry-dead plants. She hesitated under the eaves of the house, listening for the slightest sound, before edging her way around to the back.

Through a window, she saw her father sitting bent over the

bed on which the woman lay. Her face was gaunt in the dim, flickering light of an oil lamp, her eyes closed. A shadow had fallen across his face and Rosine couldn't make out his expression. She bit hard on her bottom lip, but it didn't stop the palpitations in her chest. *I must go. What if he sees me?*

The woman opened her eyes. She looked at him and nodded. He slipped his hand under the pillow and lifted her head. He held the glass as she drank. With the edge of the sheet, he dabbed the cloudy white liquid from her lips. He held her hands and leaned forward to kiss her forehead, her cheek, her mouth, her forehead again.

As he drew his hand down over her face and closed her eyes, Rosine clamped both hands over her mouth. *It's over.* She ran home.

———

Rosine left her umbrella and muddy shoes on the mat by the kitchen door and her wet shawl over the back of a chair. In the guest room, she unzipped her dress, undid her bra and slipped off her white cotton panties. She stepped into the shower and lathered her body with Merlese's creamy, scented soap. She was careful, though, not to wash the blood off her lower lip.

In front of the full-length mirror, she let Merlese's soft, white towel fall around her ankles. Her fingertips traced slow circles around her shoulders, down over the perfect roundness of her breasts, like silken globes, tweaking her nipples until they puckered, down over the smooth curve of her belly, and down. A delicious shiver swept through her.

She slipped into her underwear. Her dress had begun to dry, so before putting it on, she cupped her hand under the bathroom tap and patted wet patches onto the shoulders and around the hemline.

She curled up in his armchair, very still, with her arms wrapped around her knees. The commotion in her head was silent now, her mind empty of everything and everyone. The fresh glow inside her seemed to be melting her body, but her heartbeat was strong. She gazed at the shelf with the family Bible and the Home Sweet Home lamp, and the shelf above with her row of teas. She closed her eyes but stayed awake, listening. The early morning light was glowing through the kitchen window when she heard his footsteps. She stretched like a cat in the sun.

He stepped over her shoes and frowned. "Hmmm, you mouth bleeding." He ran the corner of a kitchen towel under the tap. She stuck out her bottom lip for him to dab it, but he handed her the towel. "Here use this." There was no expression on his face.

He removed her shawl, still damp, from the back of the chair and sat with his elbows on the table, his eyes half-closed. There were sweat stains across the front of his dark blue T-shirt and under the arms. He pinched the bridge of his nose between his thumb and forefinger, a sure sign that he had a headache coming on. She heated the tea she'd made with bay leaf, ginger and other herbs and put a cup in front of him. He didn't drink it, but he had to be breathin in the steam as he opened his mouth twice, as if to tell her something important. But all he said was, "You best take off that wet dress before you catch cold."

Even good men like Papa sometimes get confused by outside women. People will talk, embarrassing for him, but not for long. He knows that I know, and never will he let it happen again.

As he stood, Rosine linked her arm in his and guided him to his room. It was like holding an empty sleeve, but she would soon have him back to normal.

NO BACK DOOR

The man strides towards the sea. He favours his left leg and avoids the soft sand that would suck in his bare feet and slow him down. He swipes his forearm across his brow and scans the waves, from left to right and back. He looks up at the sky and tilts his head, as if he's sniffing the air or listening for something. He seems oblivious to the setting sun's golden shimmer from horizon to shore.

His body is like a stick of burnt cane, jointed at the knees and shoulders. There is no hair on his head; his beard is white. He wears brown cutoff pants and a sleeveless off-white T-shirt, with *Save the Turtles* faded on the back. He carries a homemade fishing rod and a blue bucket. He anchors the bucket just above the tidemark.

To his left, beyond the breaking waves, a dark rippling shape appears, like hundreds of leaves fluttering under water. In three swift paces, he's there, wading in up to his thighs. He sweeps his line in an expert arc, almost careless. A moment later, he whips it out with a small, silver fish attached.

He turns to his right with a wide-open smile to the two children sitting well back on the beach, next to a pile of washed-up driftwood, away from the manchineal tree and its skin-blistering apples. He holds up the rod with the fish spinning and thrashing, its scales catching the sun's dying rays. His other hand, palm forward, fingers splayed, warns the children to stay where they are. The sea has no back door.

The little girl claps her hands and wriggles her toes in the sand. She wears a yellow dress and has a white ribbon in her hair. The boy, in frayed khaki pants, is taller but just as bony. He punches the air with his fist, but the man is busy reloading bait.

Out goes the line and back it comes with another fish, and another, each looking larger than the one before. With a flick of his wrist, the man twists fish off the hook and tosses them into the bucket.

The boy covers the girl's feet with handfuls of sand and pats them down, as if he's building a pair of heavy boots. He decorates one and gives her broken bits of coral stone and seashell for the other, strands of seaweed to tie as laces. With a piece of driftwood, he draws a tight circle around her in the sand.

He crawls towards the bucket; it must be half full by now. His shadow traces a sundial arrow to the girl. She kicks off her sand-boots and crosses the circle.

The man looks up, over his left shoulder. A dark cloud looms over the manchineal tree. Back out goes his line. He jerks it up. Nothing. He adds more bait and flings it again, the small lead weight taking the hook into deeper water. Nothing again.

He looks to his right and lifts a hand to shade his eyes. The bright flash, caught in the sun's last blink, in the foam of a higher breaking wave, is like a yellow umbrella with black spokes. He turns sharply to where he'd instructed the children to stay. He drops his rod and pushes towards the shore against the heavy undertow. His feet sink into the wet sand, his right leg buckles. He scrambles up and crashes back into the surf, his hands working like paddles now. He grabs one spoke-arm, and the other.

———

The man squats on the sand, silhouetted against the darkening sky. He folds her arms and her legs, draws her limp yellowness into his own rib cage, his dripping beard, his dread-knot shoulders. His mouth that blew breath into hers presses against her forehead, his fist that panic-pounded her back has slowed to a mindless thump, thump as he rocks her body – as if he neither feels the rain pelting and lashing his back nor cares that the sea has claimed his fishing rod too.

Like a saltwater trail over the sand, her white ribbon points to the boy, soaked and slumped over the blue bucket of dead fish.

EVELYN

There it is. Evelyn bends forward and winces as the pain stabs her lower back. She clasps the broom handle with both hands and leans heavily against it. Right there between the floor boards under his bed, glowing up at her like a milky-white eye. "Aunt Ev, we lost a pendant," he had told her. "A pearl with a loop, about so big." He held up his manicured index finger and thumb, about half an inch apart. She remembered him then as a baby, how that same finger used to curl around hers as if he'd never let go.

"You hearing me?" he barked.

"Yes. You jump me, Master Arnold." This is what she calls him these days. "I going look for it good." But she was thinking, *We – who is this we? How he could disrespect his mother so, bringing a woman into her house and she pass 'way not yet two months?*

There it is, yes.

Evelyn groans as she hauls herself up. A knife, she needs a knife. She pads on her flat, bare feet across the bedroom floor towards the kitchen. *No, a knife might scratch it. Nail file, that should do it.* She rummages through her bag – keys, umbrella, a thick slice of coconut bread wrapped in foil, her purse, the cellphone her son sent, down to the roll of three fifty-dollar bills tied with a rubber band she's saving to fix her leaking roof. It's under her collection of empty plastic bottles and plastic bags – the ones that zip-lock tight.

She places her bag on the bed, and his pillows on the floor, one for each knee. She inserts the nail file between the floorboards, under the pearl pendant, and levers. It's jammed. Sweat drips from her forehead into her eyes, down her neck, soaking the front of her dress. Her knees burn. She sinks onto the floor, straightens her legs and leans against the bed.

She reaches towards the bedside cabinet. Inside is a bottle of
Rémy Martin XO Fine Champagne Cognac he hides, still about
three-quarters full. *He won't notice.* She wipes her face and hands
with the skirt of her dress, opens the bottle, lifts it to her lips and
takes a sip, and one more. She reaches for her bag, removes one
of the plastic bottles and decants some of the golden liquid into
it. Her hands are steady now.

She is tired, tired of all the mopping, washing wares and
scouring pots, chasing cockroaches and spraying mosquitoes;
dusting around his do-not-touch accounting files, and his mother's Christmas cards still there on a crocheted doily; sweeping up
black-dog hairs; scraping his leftovers from the night before into
the garbage. She mutters to herself about how, at her age, she
should be home cooling out and watching *Days of Our Lives* but
here she is, day after day, still wearing an apron, sucking salt,
feeling pain hot in her joints, pressure throbbing behind her eyes,
her calloused hands and fungus fingernails that never get the
chance to heal. Swollen feet and her knees, oh her knees, the
bending down to scrub the two baths and two toilets, the getting
back up.

She hums hymns and pushes her tongue through the gaps
between her teeth as she dusts the photos, a row of six in matching
black, lacquered frames on a shelf in his bedroom. Photos of
Arnie in his high chair, sweet boy with his bunny teeth, up to
Master Arnold in his graduating gown and hat, and his moustache. She traces his outline with her fingers, the little boy she
used to comfort when his father tried to toughen him up, punch
him in the belly, cuff him on the back of his head, calling after him
as he cried, "Run to Mama, boy, run to Mama." But it was her he
ran to and she would stop whatever she was doing – peeling yams
or chopping onions – wipe her hands and hold him, his cheek on
her breast, like it used to be with her own son before he got into
secondary school and into long pants, too much man too soon.
Rocking Arnie, patting his sobbing back while his own mother
was out, busy doing whatever.

Evelyn runs the duster over his clock radio. *Lord, Lord, midday
already. Break time.*

She looks down to check that his dog is chained in the yard before putting her feet up on his long chair on the back gallery. Crazy, red-eye, black dog, with shark-teeth and a growl like thunder. She relaxes with her tea, sweetened with condensed milk, and her coconut bread, fanning her face with a table mat. On other days, she brings cassava pone, banana bread or a jam turnover. Sometimes, she has some of the Rum 'n Butter Fudge he keeps in a tin at the back of the fridge, just a sliver. She can cool out for an hour, maybe longer, now that his mother has passed and there's no more calling, "Evie, Evie" from the bedroom every minute.

Sylvie was her friend from school-days. Like sisters they were, sharing their secrets, giggling so much that the teachers separated them. There was that Sunday they got sent home from church when dotish old Father Luke forgot to put in his false teeth and was thssing and spitting all through his sermon, and a wood-dove flew in and shat on the pulpit, just missing his head, and he continued preaching as if nothing happened. Lord have mercy, they actually wet themselves laughing, both of them.

But things changed – Sylvie marrying the insurance man with his pink tie and matching kerchief sticking out of his top pocket; and his white, new brand Honda car driving past her at the bus stop – and she, Evelyn, and her big belly, left standing there. Her one mistake. The older girls saying it was the hottest, sweetest thing, the boy pressuring. She telling him, "No, I not ready," and he mocking, "Little girl, little girl, why you playing so hard to get? Everybody doing it," and she telling him, "No is no," and he saying, "Trust me," and, "If I can't get it from you, I going find some other body." You see how life is? One mistake, when you too young to know what going on. Like a rag doll against the wall of the outside toilets at school. She can't even remember his name.

You could band your belly all you like, but soon it must show. She can still hear her teachers' voices as she picked up her books and left school. "Throwing your life away. Another good girl gone bad." Her mother crying shame. Her father said nothing, but she felt his heavy let down.

He used to toss her into the air, his "sugar-cakes", calling "fly-butter-fly", swinging her upside-down by her feet, treats in his pocket – a tamarind ball, a white frangipani flower, a pink hair ribbon. Her mother warned, "You spoilin' she." Evelyn can't forget his sad eyes avoiding hers, his one and only girl-child.

The tea and bread and brandy are warm and mushy in her belly. Ten more minutes, some Limacol on her head-tie, and she'll be just fine. She closes her eyes and turns her thoughts to the evening last week when the man-himself turned up. She had dialled Prestige Home Construction from the Yellow Pages and there he was on her doorstep.

"Charlie, is you? What you doing here?" Charles "Headlights" Brathwaite – she remembered the good-time easy boy, spicy aftershave, strutting like a rooster. Plenty style and sweet talk, asking her to come ride on the back of his motorbike. But she had her baby son then, and no way was she going to mess up her life again.

"Miss Evelyn," he said, flashing those big-bright eyes and bowing as he held up a bulging tool bag in one hand, an open bottle of Banks Beer in the other. "I come to fix you roof."

So said, so done, and she paid the bill. But he came back and repaired the light over her front door, the leaking tap in the kitchen, the floor board in her bedroom and the plug on the microwave her son ordered from Courts for her last birthday. His jokes made her laugh like a young girl and forget all the things that were vexing her spirit – the money troubles, high blood pressure and her son so far away. It was good to have a man about the house. And yes, she let him rub her feet with Bengies Balsam – deep strokes with strong hands soothing away all her bad dreams of black dogs and her elephant feet, and all the rest of her teeth dropping out.

The phone is ringing. She must have dozed off. *Enough of these foolish thoughts, like you mussee drunk.* She heaves herself up, squeezes her yam-feet into her slippers and scrambles to reach the phone, glancing at the kitchen clock – nearly two o'clock already.

It's him, humbugging her. "My yellow polo-shirt needs a button sewing back on. And don't forget to take in the sheets. You forgot last week." *And next you going want me to press the damn sheets too? What it is I am now?* She hadn't much minded helping out Sylvie – like friends should do. But this for her son is more like domestic servant, nanny to a grown man – shame on him.

She checks the rice and peas – nearly done – lays out his plate, knife and fork with a white linen napkin, opens the oven door – chicken ready – turns off the gas.

Her son used to call every Sunday but, these days, he mostly buys things for her. Big man now, busy in London with his own family. She went there once, met his wife, clinging like love-vine – all blond and gold ring, sending Christmas cards with reindeer and robins, with love and hugs XXX. Plenty Bajan men would run from women so, all the way from Bridgetown to North Point. *Why he couldn't stand home and marry his own kind?* And those two boy-children of his running about, the yelling and the backchat. She couldn't stand for that; she would have to put two licks in their tail and, most likely, end up in an English police cell. No, she was better off where she was, making do with her little savings so she won't have to go on welfare. And maybe Charlie there lending a hand. *Hmmm, you best hold strain,* she told herself. *How many things in life you wish for ever happen?*

Rice and peas ready, she takes out lettuce, tomatoes and cucumber from the fridge, and cuts them up. She must remind him to buy more of that fancy blue-cheese dressing.

These days there's not much to do in Sylvie's bedroom, just dust a bit. She has time; he won't get home 'til after four. Sitting on the bed, she looks around the room she's cleaned for over thirty years, ever since the day Sylvie phoned, telling her she must come visit, cool and light like an invitation to afternoon tea. It wasn't an invitation, not even a question – as if Sylvie knew she wouldn't refuse. They hadn't spoken since Arnie was born, and her husband dead, sudden so. But he left them well-provided-for, according to Sylvie. The visits became a little helping out with this and that, bathing Arnie and changing his diaper, then some cooking and cleaning. And all the while, Sylvie trying to give her gifts – a jar of body lotion, a box of three lavender soaps, a pair of linen napkins with lace around the edge and blue embroidered flowers in one corner. But she never accepted a thing.

One day, as she was leaving, she saw an envelope with her name on it on the kitchen table. Evelyn folded her arms and narrowed her eyes. She turned away and put on her shoes and hat, thinking that things were a bit tight, what with her own son growing so fast, needing new school shoes and extra lessons and wanting his own cricket bat, and her meeting-turn money not stretching. She pursed her lips, looked up at the ceiling as she put the envelope into her bag and called out, "Sylvie, I gone."

"Get home safe," Sylvie replied from her bedroom. "See you tomorrow."

Evelyn leans forward and rubs her sore knees. She sniffs. That musty smell of Sylvie still clings – the spring-flower-bouquet air freshener could never spray it away. She pulls back the heavy brocade curtains and the white net ones, and opens the bedroom windows. *How life could turn and spin you round when you least expect?* Who could believe that she would be working for Sylvie, and Sylvie paying her; she staying all these years, moving in for the night nursing when Sylvie got sick. The two of them together again and Sylvie going on about her happy childhood, her Easter bonnet with yellow ribbons, and her being Mary in the nativity play and winning first prize at the singing contest. And Evelyn half-listening, feeling like a blackbird keeping company with a yellow, squawking parrot.

She stared at Sylvie's bottles of pills on the bedside table and thought back to the carbolic lotion, coconut oil, aloes and castor oil she had as a child, and the time the girl from up the gap disappeared and they never found her; and the one from her class at school who screamed and screamed in the girls' toilet – thought she was bleeding to death because nobody told her what to expect. *How my memories could be so different?*

Holding hands, Sylvie bawling as the pain got worse, praying together, waiting for Sylvie to sleep. She didn't last long. Her back like a bent fork, she'd shuffle to the bathroom, calling, "Arnie, Arnie", and him out someplace else. And then her mouth could only shape words, her tongue coated with scum, chicken soup and cream of wheat running down her chin, hair like dry-season bush, fingers like black coral scrunching up the bedcover. She was all bones and sagging skin, like a stained sheet, the sickness drawing her lifeblood until the day she took her last rattle breath. Sixty-seven years and gone, and Evelyn there to close her sunken eyes and pray for her soul. *And me, the fallen one – me still living.*

Evelyn feels better. She could manage the steps down to the yard to go take in the sheets. The dog is in the kennel, out of the hot sun. *Him and that dog. You could never know people.* One morning, she'd arrived early and seen him sitting on the top step, his back to her, the dog's head in his lap, murmuring soft words, scratching behind its ears, its red tongue hanging out.

She remembers the pendant. *Ice pick, that will do it. Stick it into the loop at the top, ease it up, easy now, yes.*

Success. She fills the washbasin in his bathroom with hot water, adds a drop of disinfectant and soaks the pendant. It belongs to some slut who wears God knows what cheap scent and greasy face-cream. She folds it gently in his soft white towel. In the mirror, she smiles a secret smile at the pearl sitting, oh so pretty, in the hollow at the base of her throat above the cross she wears on a silver chain. *Lord, lead me not into temptation.*

"I only need you one day a week now," he had said, less than a month after his mother passed, his little moustache like a black toothbrush twitching, "but my colleague, Mrs. Edghill, she can give you three days. So, here on Monday, by her Wednesday, Thursday, Friday," holding up those fingers of his – one, two, three, four – "then you get Tuesday off," wagging his clever little thumb, like it was a favour he was doing her; like she had no say; like a house could clean itself in one day. She didn't confront him. He would only stress her out, turn her words against her in that way he had. So, she kept her thoughts to herself. She needed the money for a new fridge. At Mrs. Edghill's it was more of the same, except there were the four children's socks to pick up and wet towels dumped on the bathroom floor, and school uniforms to press, and hamburgers to fry.

She was in his kitchen ironing one morning when she heard him on his cellphone in his bedroom telling someone – had to be Mrs. Edghill, "She's been working here from since I was small, and she never broke a thing, not a cup, not one glass. You could believe that? Really?" That was when she spat on the iron, *pssst*, before pressing and folding his yellow shirt so the missing button wouldn't show. *Yellow*, she thought, *is good for egg yolks or cornmeal or sunflowers, but for a man's shirt? Cuh dear, no.*

After he'd left for the office to do his counting-thing, sunshine boy posing in his tight, shiny-grey suit and shoes so long he must have to go upstairs backwards, she let a plate slip into the kitchen sink. The following Monday, a brandy glass – careful not to cut her fingers as she wrapped fragments of china and splinters of glass in newspaper and shoved them to the bottom of the garbage, the thrill streaking through her. No, she never broke a thing, not her.

It was around that time, too, she started bringing the plastic bottles and bags. And why shouldn't she? Nothing big, nothing that would last, just things she'd never have bought for herself, a little white sugar or rice – Uncle Ben's, no picking – one or two Earl Grey tea bags, a sprig of grapes, that blue-cheese dressing or olive oil – extra virgin, if you please. And sometimes a tip of orange blossom honey that tasted so good on her salt bread on mornings. She would never have done anything so when Sylvie was still living and they prayed together. But these days, she told herself, *Girl, what go round don't always come back round, sometimes you got to make it happen.*

He hadn't said a thing. But what if he'd been checking, marking the level of brandy in the bottle? What if he'd counted his costs and losses, calculating with those fingers of his, then cut her time down to one day a week. Her spirit is telling her this cannot go on. She knows it very well.

She sits at his kitchen table, the pearl pendant nestling in the cupped palm of her hand, like a humming bird egg. She should call him. She starts dialling, but changes her mind. After all, he has told her to call only in emergencies.

She reaches for the notepad and pen he leaves for her to write reminders for him to buy food, or call the man to fix the washing machine. Dear Master Arnold, she writes, and crosses it out. What to say to this man who should be like family to her, but knows nothing about respect, who needs a full-time nursemaid, who can only talk to dogs? She knows exactly how to end it: *In memory of your dear mother and my best friend, Aunty Evelyn.* But she crumples the note into her bag with the plastic bottles and the zip-bags, empty now.

The chime of the kitchen clock breaks into her thoughts. It's four o'clock – she must leave before he gets back. She unclasps her chain and removes the cross. Her swollen fingers are deft as she threads the silver chain through the loop on the pearl pendant and fastens it around her neck. It's time to go home. She will leave his sheets on the line.

STILL

Kenneth

October all over, so they say. But Sonia looks across the rooftops to the sky and sea merged into an ash-grey veil that hides the horizon. Another storm on its way. She grips the arms of her rocking chair and leans forward. Ben was right, the boy could never have been hers. And him gone, too. Heaven help her, she should have let him be.

A while passes before the sharp throbbing in her temples eases and she can sit upright. She lays her pinstriped, grey jacket across her knee on top of her clutch bag and removes her black, high-heeled shoes. She stretches her knee and looks at the scab below it. If only other scars could heal as well. She twists her wedding ring around her finger and lowers her gaze from the top step to the front gate and visualises him there – his little bare feet curling around the wrought iron bars, the fingers of one hand clinging to the top, the other hand clutching a grubby piece of paper.

That Saturday morning, Sonia had been in the kitchen sipping ginger tea, not yet out of her dressing gown. She heard the child's voice call from outside, opened her front door and blinked into the light as she looked down at him.

"I come for you to sign this." He held out the paper.

She put her hands on her hips. "Good morning, young man."

"Morning, miss." She noted his picky hair, faded T-shirt and frayed short pants, his skinny legs and scraped knees. His mouth was too big for his face. The only time kids like him ventured into her neighbourhood was to steal mangoes or retrieve flyaway kites. They never came alone. He looked at her with eyes like black marbles about to pop out of their sockets.

"What is your name, young man?"

"Kenneth, miss." He pronounced it *Kennef*.

"KenneTH, TH, TH. You must learn how to speak properly to get on in this world."

"KenneTH," he said, sticking his tongue out, "Goodridge."

"Well, you'd better get down off the gate and come up here." He did, without hesitation, and handed her the paper. She was not accustomed to inviting anyone in off the street, never mind the likes of him.

"So, how old are you?"

"Seven years, miss, and ten months."

She was about to ask more questions when Ben arrived home from cricket practice, and came between them. He kissed her cheek. "How you feeling, love? You eat the fishcakes and bakes I fix for you?" He turned to Kenneth. "Hi, there, kiddo."

She signed the Sponsored Spell sheet. It looked official with its heading, *Holy Cross Primary School*.

The boy – what was his name? – returned a week later and announced, "I get all right. Is ten cents a word, so one hundred cents, one dollar, miss. Please."

"Hmmm. Wait there, while I get my purse," she said. "And hands out of your pockets."

Through the kitchen window, Sonia watched him pick at a scab on his foot until he lifted it, exposing the pink patch underneath, then lick his finger and nibble the scab with his front teeth. Ugh! She was still frowning as she handed him a plastic cup of mango juice with ice and a straw – and a plaster. She sat in her rocking chair watching him as he applied the plaster and drank the juice. She made him wait for his dollar.

As he scurried off, she called out, "And young man, do stop eating your scabs."

———

Three months later, he was back, ringing the front doorbell this time. "Good morning, miss, is twenty words now, two dollars."

Boldfaced as a green monkey, but there was something about the way he beamed those hungry eyes and hopped from one foot to the other that stirred an instinct in her. She told him to sit down on the step, brought him a glass of juice, asked him his name again and where he lived, and about his family.

"Hinds Gap, miss. My grandmother, she raising me."

"What about your mother?"

"She pass 'way."

"Ah. And your father, where is he?"

"Dunno," he said, and "Dunno," again when she asked what he wanted to be when he grew up.

By the time he returned the following Saturday with every word spelt correctly, Sonia had persuaded herself that he could probably do with a little help in life, just a little ease up, nothing more.

He gobbled down the cornbread and ham that Ben had left for her. She wanted to tell him not to eat so quickly, but there'd be time for that later. He fell asleep on the step, his head resting against the wall, mouth slightly open, his tongue on his bottom lip, poor baby, so still – but no, not a baby, and not still. She felt a sudden urge to bite into his arm, curled like a roll of black pudding around his knees, to lift him onto her lap, as if he were her own, and rock away all the scabby, barefoot hardship of his life. She bent over and touched his cheek with her lips. Whatever got into her?

Sonia turned quickly away as he blinked and rubbed his face with both hands. "Hold on a minute," she said. She went inside and returned with a pencil and sheet of white paper which she placed on the step. She knelt and drew the outline of the sole of his foot.

"Don't move," she said, though it was her hand shaking.

"But you tickling me, miss," he giggled and she couldn't help laughing – she hadn't laughed in months.

She rubbed off the mud smudges his foot had left on the paper. "Come back next Saturday and I'll have a surprise for you."

What was she thinking?

Ben had warned her, "Watch what you getting youself into. You doan know nothing 'bout his background."

But, I do, she thought.

Later, when Kenneth opened the box with the bright red, white-lace sneakers, his eyes nearly flew out of his head. "Whoa, wicked."

"Excuse me?"

"Sorry, miss. Thank you, miss." Clutching the box, he skipped down the steps, turned his head and smiled, a pocketful of sunshine over his shoulder.

Sonia rocks back as she remembers her Saturdays with Kenneth – over two years it lasted. She began with reading *The Wind in the Willows*, acting the parts, puffing out her cheeks for Toad, peering through half-closed eyes and moving her arms breaststroke style, fingers splayed, for Mole. "You looking like an obsocky turtle, miss," he said. So, she had to explain Mole, but he knew all about rats and crapauds. They read *Anancy, Alice in Wonderland, Peter Pan, Harry Potter* – oh dear, *Harry Potter*. And there was all that coaching she put him through, the manners and standing up straight, speaking and eating properly, no biting fingernails. What on earth had possessed her?

Ben

Sonia Browne met Ben Armstrong when they were law students. She was only eighteen, not looking to hook up with anyone, unlike the other girls in her class – strutting their stuff, flaunting breasts in low-cut tops and backsides in too-tight skirts. She knew his half-closed eyes were fixed on her from the back of the lecture room and across the carrels in the library. The creepy old man, she'd thought, though he was barely middle-aged. She focused her attention on lecture notes and legal case studies, on her future. Until the night she worked late on her coursework assignment, lost track of time and missed the last bus. "May I offer you a ride home?" he said.

She remembered all her mother's warnings about not talking to strange men, and this man had watched her like a stalker. She'd heard, too, he was married. But she had no taxi money, not like

her at all. She really had no choice. She gave directions and sat as
far from him as she could, clutching her bag of books with one
hand, the other ready to open the car door. They drove in silence,
but the engine choked, spluttered and cut out.

"Doan worry," he said, revving it up. "Safe and sure – just like
me."

Her mother's bedroom light was on. "Somebody waiting up
for you," he said, patting her arm. She muttered thanks and fled.
Later they joked about it. "May I offer?" she'd quip. "Talk about
a scared little mouse," he'd say.

Ben was forty-two when he enrolled in the Law Faculty, after
nearly twenty years as a policeman. He'd struggled to reach a
lower second, not bad for him, while she came straight from
school and soared to a first-class degree with a distinction in
Family Law. By that time, though, she was pregnant. Ben said
that he and his wife were done, and in truth the divorce was easy
– no fault, no children, no custody, no real property. So they got
it fast-tracked, and married.

The house they chose was described in the real-estate blurb as
*The family home you have been waiting for, beautifully presented with
a window to the sea. Two double bedrooms, one en suite, a spacious
living room, a well-equipped, modern kitchen and a mature garden.* It
was more expensive than they'd budgeted for and needed some
work, but Sonia loved the new residential area, the ridge with cool
breezes and the sea view. Ben was impressed by the neighbourhood watch and the walled-in garden with a julie-mango tree.
They took out a long-term mortgage.

Before they moved in, on Saturdays, while Ben played cricket,
Sonia paced from room to room with a clipboard, looking down
her long, arched nose, her slim fingers pointing out any sign of
shoddy work to an army of plumbers, painters and carpenters.
She would leave after dark, exhausted by the hammering and
drilling, cement dust and sawdust between her teeth, and the
clinging stench of paint and varnish, but determined her home
would be elegant.

"Love, you gotta slow down," Ben said.

Her feet did get a bit swollen and she was nauseous at times, but that was normal. She felt so alive. "We're both doing fine," she said, patting her bulge.

She had it all organised. The furniture and blinds were ordered by catalogue. With his arm around her shoulders as she turned the pages, Ben let her have her way. He pampered her, though sometimes she felt him wince at the prices. The honey-themed living room had an upholstered couch with purple velvet cushions and cream crocheted antimacassars, a mahogany dining table with six chairs, and a tall cabinet with a glass-fronted top for her crystal collection, and a section for Ben's liquor.

He ordered a front gate specially made to her design, the bars painted green and shaped like sugar cane, with segmented stalks and pointed blades. He attached to it a black post box with *Homestead* written on it in gold lettering. His choice. She'd have preferred a less stodgy name. He fixed a deadbolt to the kitchen door and installed burglar bars and a panic button alarm system. "No vagabonds or vermin in our home," he said. Sonia shuddered.

The nursery was her showpiece. There was a crib with a musical mobile of rainforest friends, a soft rug with dinosaurs, a chest of drawers filled with baby bottles, bibs and booties, all in blue – the ultrasound showed a son. Ben had seemed disappointed, as if he'd been expecting a girl, but only a little and not for long. In the wall cupboard were a stroller, a car seat and a high chair. On the wall above the cot was a chart with pictures of animals from Aardvark to Zebra and, on the other side of the room, shelves with brightly coloured toys for counting and testing hand-to-eye coordination, and a row of baby books.

Sonia led Ben by the hand through each room. He took such delight in her delight. He was so proud of her.

"But we could stop now?" he said.

"Yes dearest, everything is ready."

———

Ben wasn't perfect. He was good looking enough, an inch taller than Sonia in her high heels. Clean-shaven, his hair was cut short and had only a few flecks of grey. And he was fit, always rotating his shoulders and swinging his arms, jogging on the beach and

diving through the waves. There were a few coarse edges that she
tried to smooth out, like the way he held his knife and fork, sat
with his legs wide apart, cracked his knuckles, scratched his balls
and walked around the house naked. Yes, Sonia had a list.

"I am who I am," he told her.

His Christian faith seemed unshakable. He went to Sunday
morning service regularly and was a pillar of the Men's Fellow-
ship. When he forgot to take out the garbage or change a light
bulb, she would tease, "I see a rust spot on your halo." But he was
a good man. Too good for her really and, deep down, she knew
that, even then. And he had a melting touch – not that she'd
known any other – so she didn't too much mind the roughness of
his hands on her swelling breasts. They settled into a twice-a-week
rhythm that seemed to satisfy him. There was no flirting on her
part, no seduction on his, no reckless passion bursting like shooting
stars or falling off cliffs, just quiet intimacy. The kind of lovemak-
ing that would last, she thought, though she wasn't inclined to
think too far into the future. Although she didn't have Ben's faith,
Sonia believed there had to be some godlike presence to ensure
order and morality in the world. She herself was strictly monoga-
mous. From her court cases, she knew all about the trauma and
violence triggered by men, and women, stepping out.

Ben was reserved and she liked to rattle him, just a little. "So,
what made you fall in love with me?" She knew she wasn't pretty,
more like attractive in a structured kind of way. He'd just give her
hand a little squeeze. Maybe it was the vulnerability she tried to
hide that he loved. She needed someone to protect her, mostly
from herself, though he'd never tell her that.

"I never going leave you," he said.

"Promise?"

He was there for her with hugs when his ex-wife phoned and
cursed her; when her personal supervisor, Professor Powell,
hinted that he was beneath her; when her classmates twittered as
she began to show; when her own mother cried, "Shame on you
with that old man. He will leave you, too, the same way. After
everything I've done for you, you're going to kill me with this?"
With each lash against him, Sonia became more convinced that

Ben was the man for her, her rock, the soul-mate with whom she would share everything, always.

She preened like a cat as he adored her, did everything expected of a father-to-be. He rubbed away signs of stretch marks with cocoa butter, indulged her cravings for chicken livers, vanilla ice cream and pickled onions, and attended birthing classes, breathing in rhythm with her. He read book after book and showed her the pictures. "See, love, this is how she looks now."

"He," Sonia reminded him. Why was he making such a fuss? Having a baby just needed organisation. She would regulate feeding so that he'd soon be sleeping through the night and express her milk so that the nanny – they'd have to find a good one – could feed him during the day. And she'd be back in shape in less than a month with a strict diet and exercise programme. Sonia, modern super-mother.

"Hello Little Ben," he said, "Ben Two," as he caressed the baby, feeling the kicks with his hands, his cheeks, his lips. He hugged Sonia.

"Oopsie, not so tightly, dear."

Three days later, her world crashed.

She can still see the sharp outline of the nurse in her crisp white cap, and hear the three words, "Son, Still, Born", making no sense. She had struggled against their hands clenched around her arms and legs, against their words, and screamed, "*I want my baby*." But they wouldn't let her see him. Ben held her shoulders as they gave her an injection. He said nothing.

————

There are babies everywhere, so many babies. Babies at the courts, in the supermarket, on the streets in cars, in pushchairs, in the arms of their mothers. She steals quick looks from behind her dark glasses, but there is always something not quite right – girl babies, white babies – not old enough, not young enough, no sign of her nose or Ben's lazy eyes, until she realises her search is too haphazard. She must go to *The Mother and Baby Wellbeing Centre*, the private clinic for couples with money to buy babies.

The waiting room is large with yellow-brown, upright seats

for more than fifty people. She avoids eye contact and goes to a corner or the back row, never the same place twice. She doesn't go every day, or stay for too long – just lunch hours and Saturday mornings when the room is full and Ben is off playing cricket. The brochures she pretends to read advertise ultrasounds and the prevention of mother-to-child transmission of HIV, birthing and breastfeeding, immunisation and vitamin supplements, antenatal care and post-partum depression counselling – none of which she needs. She's already dealt with her own afterpains, backache and swollen feet. The bleeding has stopped and her milk has dried up. No one notices her at first, but after a time, someone must have recognised her and called Ben.

"Can't you see?" she cried, pummelling his chest. "They sold our baby, from the hospital."

Ben held her head between his hands and leant towards her so that their eyes were almost touching. "Sonia, he died. I held his body."

———

Ben lead her to the bedroom to lie down, a pill with a glass of water, stroking her forehead until merciful sleep took over from her howling, her sobbing, her whimpering. But he couldn't stop her terrifying dreams or cure the hollowness she felt, as if her insides had been sucked out, or prevent her mind going back over and over – what did she do wrong? Maybe all that work with the house, the paint fumes?

Ben bought chocolate mousse in little cups and fed her with a teaspoon as he wiped tears from her cheeks. "You didn't do nothing wrong," he told her. He built a gazebo for her in the garden, strung a hammock across it and trailed a climbing plant over the top with large yellow flowers that hung down and swayed in the breeze.

"Like tolling bells," she wailed. "Why didn't you bring him home?"

Ben massaged her feet, washed her hair, polished her black court shoes and ironed her white blouses. Somehow she held her career together, her legal public face intact, until she got home and sat hunched on the blue baby rug, numb and scarred as a coral stone statue. When Ben arrived home, her fury would burst. She shrieked, "*You* sold him. *You* wanted a girl," and cursed his God, "Vengeful, giveth and taketh it all back, every blasted thing."

"Let it out, love," Ben said. "You must let it all out."

For Sonia, there was only one way to overcome her grief. But no matter how much she pleaded, how her tears streamed, how she beat her head against his shoulder, Ben was adamant. "No. Not another baby. Not now."

"Why not?"

Ben wouldn't answer.

"When then?"

That was when she met Kenneth, and an idea began to flicker in her mind. After all, as a family lawyer, she'd come across every kind of disadvantaged child. All they needed was someone to cherish them and give them a good start in life.

———

Specks of dust bobbed in the first light of morning filtering through the bedroom windows. It was quiet except for the twittering of an early bird. Sonia knew that if she went back to sleep, he would come to her in an even more frightening image – the early morning ones were the worst. No, Little Ben, not today. She turned towards Ben, lying with his back to her, and shook his shoulder.

"Ben, darling, I have an idea."

"Mmmm."

"Ben listen, listen to me. We have to adopt Kenneth."

"What?"

"Kenneth, adopt him."

"Like you ain't do that already?"

"I mean legally. It's the only way..."

"For him, or for you?"

"...and the process is easy. I'll take care of it all."

Ben turned over and sat up. "He already got a mother."

"No, he hasn't."

"A grandmother then."

"That's not the same. And boys need fathers, too, fathers like you." Sonia's eyes blazed, her hands reached out.

Ben grabbed her wrists. "God help us, Sonia, nuff of this madness." He flung back the sheet. "He is not one of you child support cases."

She heard the toilet flush, heard him brush his teeth and gargle, watched him put on a shirt, shorts and trainers. He looked down at her. "Where he living?"

Sonia wanted Kenneth, she wanted him more than anything. But she'd messed up. She should have circled around Ben, hinting, giving him time, until it became his idea.

"That boy is not coming back here," was all he said when he returned.

———

Ben brought home a puppy, a black Labrador. Now, what was he thinking? Bouncer, he called it. She heard him with it in the garden, "Heel, sit, fetch, good boy," every morning. She saw through the bedroom window as he pointed his finger at it, "Stay," before he paced away with its bowl of food. It slobbered pools until he called, "Come," and it scrambled forward, falling over itself to please.

"Do we really need a police dog?" she asked. "How big is it going to get?"

He chided her for the careless way she left money lying around and installed a safe.

"Treating me like a child then, Officer Armstrong?"

He brought home baked pork or chicken, macaroni pie or rice and peas and stood over her at the kitchen table.

"So we force-feeding now, Warden Armstrong?" Tough love until, even for him, it was too much. Ben, the great fixer of locks, bars and alarms, could not fix her heartache. He signed a three-year contract as a legal advisor on Caribbean issues with the Metropolitan Police in London.

"Double what I making now," he said. "It going help with the mortgage. And pay off the bills," as if they were all her fault.

She knew he'd been planning to leave her all along, like her mother had told her.

"Right then, go," she said, "and take your useless, worn-out sperm with you." How could she?

———

Ben phoned every Sunday at four o'clock, her time. He told her that the beer was warm, that his doorbell chimed like Big Ben, that his landlady was from Ireland. There were so many questions she wanted to ask – How old is your landlady? Is she pretty? How are you dealing with your grief? Do you miss me?

"Is it cold?" she asked.

"Not so bad," he said. "I got a new coat and gloves."

She didn't tell him that she dabbed his aftershave between her breasts at night; that she was adrift without him.

"So, you feeling better?"

"Yes, fine," she said. "Busy, you know." He's never needed me, she thought.

She didn't tell him about her black holes and rock bottoms; the palpitations, trembling, cold sweats, curling up on the kitchen floor in full-blown panic. There were weekends when she couldn't move from the bed and lay behind drawn curtains in a foetal position, clutching Ben's pillow in her skinny arms, low moans escaping her lips, tired – so very, very tired.

There were nightmares – a baby's head bald as a soft-boiled egg with the top sliced off, yellow-blood yolk spilling over. And always reshaping into his body on a hospital bed – still.

Ben came home for Christmas and saw for himself how she was. Sonia knew he wanted to keep her at home, but she insisted that they attend the Law Society New Year dinner – not his thing, but important for her career to be there. She fixed his cufflinks and straightened his tie, and covered up her protruding collar bones with the bright crimson pashmina shawl, his gift. She linked her arm under his as they circulated.

Professor Powell greeted them. "Do call me Carmeta, now that you've graduated." She wore a long, clinging yellow dress, overflowing the plunge neckline, totally inappropriate for the occasion, they agreed. Sonia can't remember about what or with whom they chatted. It was a long night and she overdid the mix of cocktails, white wine, red wine and desert wine on her empty stomach. He had to prop her up as she teetered on her high heels, drive her home before further embarrassment, and carry her comatose through the gate, up the steps and into bed.

He threw out all the bottles of liquor in the glass-fronted cabinet, organised his cousin, Dr. Horace Blackman, to see her and went back to London.

"What happened to 'never going leave you'?" Sonia said, but she was thinking, *Why doesn't he just shut up and go?*

Dr. Blackman, tall and thin with a sharp nose, reminded her of an egret. He came for an hour every Saturday morning. "Such a caring man," she told Ben on the phone. They sat in her living room, he twiddling his pen as he asked intrusive questions and prescribed sedatives and stimulants, calming downers and happy uppers. Baby blues syndrome, he called it.

But Sonia rather liked the manly way he cleared his throat and, after all, he did come to her home discreetly. She told him that mornings were no longer convenient and could he come in the evening instead? Then, she offered rum or might he prefer brandy? With coconut water? She batted her eyelashes – she'd watched her classmates at it. She patted the space beside her on the couch, but would have backed off in a hurry if he'd so much as touched her hand. Ah Sonia, monogamy, safe and sound.

He referred her to a female colleague. "A younger psychiatrist might be better for you." She never went, no way. Word might get around and that would never do.

Kenneth

With perfect timing, Ben back in London and appointments with Dr. Blackman over, Kenneth returned. They resumed their Saturday sessions at her kitchen table. After reading for an hour or so, she to him, he to her, it was time for etiquette, just the basics. Table manners first: "Wash your hands; now lay out the knives and forks for fish and meat, soup spoons and desert spoons; napkin on your lap, not under your chin; elbows off the table and keep them in."

She placed two table mats under his arms. "That's it and no slouching." As if she couldn't help herself. Just like her own mother, truth to tell.

She took him into her living room, "Shoes off, please," and showed off her crystal. "This one is for brandy; these with stems are for red wine and white wine; this one for champagne, a flute, so that you know the right way, Kenneth."

She handed him a glass. "Hold it up to the light, careful now, see the rainbow colours?" He cupped it in his two hands, shaking a little, as if he'd been given a newborn baby to hold. She didn't take him into the nursery, though.

Kenneth helped out, doing whatever little thing she asked. He set up a kitchen garden, worked hard at it, pulling out weeds and putting down slug pellets. He presented her with fresh lettuces, sweet cherry tomatoes and bunches of parsley with a flourish and a bow, "Your Majesty," he said as she curtseyed. "Thank you, my Prince."

"You tie up the dog, miss?" he always asked before going outside. So she got rid of it. She would tell Ben, when next he called, that it got tick fever and had to be put down or that it escaped when the plumber, or the postman, left the gate open.

They had fun times, too. He impressed her by performing card tricks with her crimson pashmina draped over his shoulders, a straw for a wand, a bold glint in his eyes. Together, they listened for the ice cream van piping out *Home, Home on the Range*, and indulged in Bico's banana split sundae, then cookies and cream – Double Delight.

"You could call me Aunty Sonia," she said. But he never did.

One Saturday, she took him by the hand and pointed to the mango tree. "Look, Kenny, julies; you could climb up and pick them. Take some home with you."

"No, miss, my grandmother would get vex."

"But I am giving you permission."

Kenneth shook his head and looked at her in that way of his when he was about to do something brazen and wasn't sure of her reaction. He lifted his T-shirt slowly, then flipped it up. A scar, like a giant centipede, crawled over his ribs. "Hole in my heart," he said, as if he were proud of it.

"Oh, my poor baby." Sonia was sure her heart skipped a beat. As she held her arms open to him, he stiffened and stepped back.

"My grandmother tell me to don't show you," he said and yanked down his T-shirt.

———

Sonia met her only once when she presented her outsize self at the gate, dressed in her Sunday best cream satin, corsets squeezing her sweaty breasts up under her chin, looking out from beneath a pink parasol. "Mistress Armstrong, I is Kenneth grandmother…"

"Good morning," Sonia said looking down from her top step.

"… and I come to speak with you." She stood there until Sonia descended and they faced each other across the gate. The old woman's scrunched up face was tilted slightly and turned to one side. Her left eye was clouded over.

"I come to tell you that Kenneth reading good, good now. He's read to me 'pon a evening. From the Bible. Not them witchy books, that got children riding 'bout on broomsticks."

"But it's only a story."

"No, m'am, it ain' good to fill a child mind with that foolishness." She rapped her gnarled fingers on the gate. "And he doan like that black dog you got out there in you yard."

"The dog has gone."

"And another thing, no climbing up in trees…"

"I know about that," Sonia said. "He showed me." She watched for a reaction.

"Hmmm. So, you got to get some other body to pick you mangoes. And he got to be back by twelve o'clock, so he could eat home." She hooked the handle of her umbrella under her arm, removed a yellowish washcloth from her bag, wiped the sweat from her forehead and neck. "Lord have mercy, this heat killing me."

Oh, no, Sonia thought, she wants to come inside. But the woman stepped back and sniffed. "Just so we understand one another. Good day to you." She trudged down the road, her umbrella and backside swinging in opposite directions.

Not a word of thanks, but so much wisdom in her one eye, knowing very well that Sonia would continue to teach Kenneth. That her own plan for her grandson was unfolding.

———

Sonia dragged herself from Mondays to Fridays, through case after case of divorce, domestic violence and child abuse, immersing herself in other people's troubles. She lived for Saturdays, when her kitchen was transformed into a playground, with Kenneth. Who said learning couldn't be fun? This was her own special project – her lifeline, truth to tell. And Ben would never find out. She blocked the past and refused to think ahead. One day at a time.

On Sundays, she rested, though it was more like collapsing into bed. One morning, though, she heard a heavy thumping sound, like giant footsteps coming into the bedroom. Not another nightmare – this was real. She lay with her thumb on Ben's panic button, eyes wide open, not daring to move. There it was again, *thump, thump, thump*, but with a kind of crunching sound, and coming from the garden. She grabbed her dressing gown.

At the kitchen door, she peered at the figure squatting by the lettuces. "What on earth are you doing? It's Sunday."

Kenneth stood up. He had a large rock-stone in his hand. "The African snails come back, miss." He pointed to the slimy, brown mess at his feet.

She gagged. "How many times must I tell you, if you mash them, they'll just drop all their eggs, hundreds of them." She shook her finger at him. "Put-them-in-the-bucket-with-Clorox."

"The Clorox done."

"So why didn't you tell me?" She threw her hands up. "You'd better go now."

He looked down at the rock and the mess, as she shut the kitchen door, and forgot Ben's deadbolt lock again, and went back to bed. And slept – the sweet relief of floating away on a white cloud. But the cloud darkened and thickened and turned inside out and there he was, but this time there was a scar across his little chest that burst wide open, his insides pulsing and spitting blood as she rushed to grab the flaps of his skin to fold back over the hole in his heart, screaming for that nurse. But no one came to stitch him up.

———

Sonia willed herself not to go to Kenneth's home. Somehow, she knew he'd be back, that his grandmother was just stringing her along. Three long Saturdays passed before she heard him open the gate.

"So, your grandmother allowed you come back?"

"She tell me bring this for you." He placed a black plastic bag on the step, took out an enamel bowl and lifted the lid with a flourish. "Ta dah. She say how you fall 'way and you must eat." He stood back, eyeing her, chewing his thumbnail. "It name rundown, got in cassava and green banana. My grandmother say to eat it from the bowl, with a spoon."

Sonia couldn't speak, not even to correct his English or threaten to rub pepper-sauce on his thumb. She could only blink and nod and try to swallow, like a fish gulping air. The aroma of coconut milk and spices was irresistible, surviving as she had been on tinned sardines and Eclipse biscuits, and ginger tea to relieve the gas. It was as if every one of her taste buds had come back to life, making her drool, get down on her hands and knees and stick her head in the bowl, stuff her mouth full, like Ben's dog.

And so, the deal was set. Kenneth would soon be ten and was due to sit the Common Entrance Examination. It was serious lessons now, no more fish forks and napkins, no more kitchen garden, no more fun and games. His grandmother sent him with his homework and past exam papers. Sonia supervised and marked. As his grades crept up, from 37 to 52 to 86 percent, she clapped her hands, though her heart was no longer in it. So much for all-round personal development, reduced to précis and pronouns, punctuated with yet more chicken curry, corn soup and pepper pot. The bowls of food kept coming. Grandmother Goodridge was in charge.

Kenneth passed for Harrison College. His arithmetic result wasn't so good, but his new English vocabulary carried him through. He showed off his uniform to Sonia, standing to attention on the top step in his khaki shorts and shirt, a little on the big side, but sharply pressed, and epaulettes in maroon and gold. A tight grin stretched across his face, but the expression was one she'd never seen before in his eyes, almost as if he were dreading it.

And that was that, all over, end of story. She'd served her purpose. "For him, or for you, Sonia?" Ben had asked. And yes, if the truth be known, for her too. She was coping, not jumping at every sound or weeping anytime, anywhere. She was sleeping through the night and eating well enough. Hunger strike done, Ben.

———

Two years passed before Sonia saw Kenneth again. It was when her house was broken into. That kind of news spread like cane-fire and he arrived in no time. He found her slumped on her living room carpet, beside the overturned cabinet, amid shards of glass and crystal.

He sat down beside her. She lifted the hem of her dress to show him a sliver embedded under her knee. "You doan need to look," he said, covering with one hand as he whipped it out with the other. Blood ran down her leg onto the carpet, oozing under his hand pressed over the wound, a hand so much bigger, with fingernails ragged and bitten down. His sinewy bare feet were nothing like the little foot she'd traced. He smelt like Ben's socks after cricket practice. A child no longer. What had she expected?

The bleeding stopped.

"You s'posed to get stitches. Like me, only not so many."

"And you could be a doctor, only you look as if you've left school. And next you're going to spend your days with the boys on the block, harassing girls in school uniform?" She spoke as if the pain in her knee was driving her.

He pulled his hand from under hers and turned towards her. She couldn't read the expression in his dull, sunken eyes.

"Will you wait with me, please?"

"Yeah, miss. I accustomed. You always like to make me wait."

Together they looked at the broken glass. "Who could do this? And why?" She thought back on recent cases of men she had prosecuted, who'd been found guilty of beating their women or backsliding on child support payments. Men out for revenge?

"Cause them couldn't find no money, nor nuffin' else to take. So, them mussee get mad," he said.

So, Ben was wrong. She should have left some money lying around, or some jewellery. She should have checked that the kitchen door was locked.

"I should have kept the dog," she said.

"Nah, my grandmother say them big black dogs got the devil in them."

"And what do you think?"

"Dunno."

"Excuse me?" Sonia raised her eyebrows.

He laughed. "My grandmother say that you is like my broughtupsy godmother." He emphasised the Ds – gran-Duh-mother, go-Duh-mother.

Godmother, she thought. Yes, good enough.

"Mmmm, Kennef, yuh could talk real good when yuh ready." She patted his arm. She was about to comment on his black T-shirt with *RECKLESS* written across the front and what looked like a skull in red, but stopped herself. Ah Sonia, at last.

"You going call you husband? My grandmother say he shoulda come back, long time."

It was a while before Sonia could speak. "And what else does she say?"

"That you been living in a dark place, like Mole under the ground, only she know that you not blind." He reached for a piece of crystal and held it up to the light. "See, you still got a rainbow."

"Yes, Kenny dear. Come, help me up." He cupped her elbow as she hobbled to the kitchen, regulating her breathing against the pain. She held his hand under the tap, washed off her blood and let it go. Well done, Sonia.

Kenneth left as the police arrived.

———

Two days later the police were back, three of them, in uniform.
They rang her doorbell at six in the morning, asked if she'd seen
Kenneth, said he was missing. It crossed Sonia's mind that the old
witch must be thinking she'd gone off her head and kidnapped
him.

They would find him, they said, and they did, later that
morning, face down in a drain in someone's backyard, soaking
wet from the rain the night before. "Fell out of a breadfruit tree,"
they said. "His heart," they said. He was only thirteen.

Mourners filled the church, spilling out into the car park, and
Sonia couldn't get near his grandmother to offer sympathies – a
relief really. The old woman sat in the front pew, her back erect,
head high under the banner proclaiming *I AM THE RESURREC-
TION AND THE LIFE* in big red letters. By the time the crowd
parted to let Sonia squeeze through, the coffin had been moved
to the front. More relief – she couldn't have looked at him, her
dearest Kenny. When the priest mentioned the breadfruit tree,
she heard a howl, "My grandson ain' no t'ief", and crept out of the
church.

Was he, though? Might it have been him? See how he slunk
away when the police arrived? And his suggestion, leave a little
money around so they won't get mad. Streetwise. Was she trying
to change him into someone he could never be? Even golden
apples like Kenny fall under the tree. Had she sent him where he
didn't belong? Did those College boys give him hell? Ben had
warned her – *For him or for you, Sonia?*

Sonia sits in her rocking chair, removes her black cloche hat
with the grey band and places it on top of her jacket, on her lap.
The clouds have built up, layer upon layer, merging into one dark
mass over her, like cement. The first large drop of rain falls on her
foot. Sonia presses her head against the back of the rocking chair
as her breath comes in gasps and her tears flow. But she will not
let the panic attack her again – breathing in-two-three, out-two-
three.

She runs through the house, dropping her hat, her jacket, her bag, her shoes, and out of the kitchen door. She smells the mustiness of the rain, hears it coming closer, pelting on galvanized roofs. It falls in huge dollops, then sheets lashing her shoulders, flooding down her face washing away her tears. She shuts her eyes as lightning streaks across the sky, puts her hands over her ears as the thunder cracks. Shaking and staggering, leaning against the gazebo, down on her knees, her head in the hammock, barefoot and drenched like him. How could she have doubted him? Her little scholar, and her saviour – still, too.

Let it all out, Ben said. And now she can.

AND BEN

Everybody got to suffer grief sometime. And, these days, they got plenty experts telling you how to get through. Five stages, according to the book I reading, and then you suppose to move on with life. But you, Sonia, you got stuck on the first one: *Denial – developing a false, preferable reality.* That is what you was doing, running 'round looking for him like crazy, wouldn't listen to me telling you that t'iefing babies does *not*, repeat *not*, happen in Barbados. Never. All my years in the police force and not one case. So, you moved to *Misplaced feelings of rage* – cussing and carrying on, letting out the vexation, but always more to come. You missed the *Bargaining* stage – Dear God, would you bring back my baby if I start believing? Not you and that!

And now you in *Depression* – telling me on the phone that you OK, you eating good and sleeping good, but I know when a person lying – all that police training I had. And when I ask how you spend the weekend, you go quiet, change the subject, never a straight answer. Sonia, I know what going on. That boy, you can't change him, and he can't fill the hole in you heart. I beg you, leave him be. And Horace telling me he done everything he could for you. And you, like you blaming me. And me here wondering if you ever going reach *Acceptance.*

For Christ's sake, Sonia, he was my son too – Ben Two. Like is only you hurting; you never did see the pain mashing up my heart, never did understand why I had to leave.

———

I am not so vex these days. My one in this London apartment with plenty time after work, I get to thinking, and you know I never was a thinker.

I remember how we used to be. That Sunday evening on the beach, and me coming out the sea, and you closing you book and the sunset on fire working magic, and me saying, "I love you." And you calling me soulmate, or something so. Me, the only one for you, everything you want in one man. You, the kind of woman that does make men gasp and forget to breathe out. Up to then, I always used to think that we men could never be with only one woman, especially us policemen. With our reputation, brains in our dicks? I still fancied other women, oh yes, Sonia, plenty young chicks come drawing up under me and some of them married, but no way was I stepping out.

And it just happen. "Supposed to be safe in the sea," I said. And, from then, me drawing you in, my butterfly on a string, don't mind my mother voice ringing in my head – "Be careful what you wish for in life; higher you climb, further you fall" – and you messing with my head, Sonia, and scorning my simple words – you mean the world to me, luckiest man in the world – my brain like a lump of yam.

But then, you telling me you pregnant and me hugging you, swinging you 'round, and shocking myself shouting, "Yes, yes, a baby. Me a father. A miracle." And not hearing you saying, "I can do something about it."

———

"There's nothing you can do," the woman said. "She needs professional help. And you need space to deal with your own grief. You should go back to London."

"Yeah, I just making things worse."

"Oh, Ben, I didn't say that." And she reaching her hand 'cross the table, fixing her eyes on me.

That was the evening after your Law Society New Year dinner that you most likely can't remember. Your professor – "Call me Carmeta" – she phoned. "Can I help in any way?" So, there we were – she and me at the Bar Noir. And she cool and clear-headed, understanding how things were. Me drinking rum, mussee my third, and my hand under hers that got on three gold rings. One of them had a big red stone catching the bar light.

That woman could listen, so I talked, not like me at all, you know that. I told her how my mind went crazy when you was expecting – how I could see you going to work in them high-high heels and falling down the front steps, belly first; and a minibus, blaring rap music, smashing into you car and driving the steering wheel in you and the baby; and a madman in court 'busing and lashing at you with a machete. I tell she how I could of kill anybody that hurt you – easy so. And every night, praying, praying, "Sweet Jesus, keep them safe."

And she saying, "Love has made you a better man."

And the rum talking now. I feel shame for telling her – your professor – that I was feeding you and washing you hair; that I couldn't handle hysterical women, saw nuff of them on the job, didn't need one in my own home; and you humbugging me for another baby, and me saying "No," and then you not letting me touch you. But I didn't tell her, leastwise I don't think so, how I jerked off in the shower, watching my sperm – "worn-out" you said it was – swirling down the drain, me hanging on to the towel rail, hanging limp.

And she leaning forward and squeezing my hand and saying, "Come, we should go now." And me looking at the bubbies like they going pop out she yellow dress.

God only knows what I was doing. And you, Sonia, you will never know. That yellow she-devil. But what she said making sense. So I gone, gone to London carrying my own grieving.

―――――

My apartment on the top floor has one bedroom and the smallest bathroom you ever did see. I could barely turn 'round in the shower. But it got a roof deck. The landlady, old Mrs. Flynn, lives on the ground floor. I try to sneak in, but the net curtain in her window twitches when I put my key in the front door lock and she catches me. "Sit yourself down and relax while I go wet the tea."

She showing me photos of her son, from a baby upwards. "Drowned he was, only sixteen, they never found him."

Jesus, how it must be, losing a son after all them years? And she shutting her green-green eyes, crossing the arms and leaning forward so I could only see the top of her cotton-white head. And me bowing, too, bowing to her pain, poor soul. "So sorry, Mrs. Flynn. Thank you for the tea, Mrs. Flynn."

Like they say, everybody supposed to come through the suffering and move on. But how? Dear God, what if you get trap all alone behind a net curtain with only photos? Without a body? And no grave to go to?

———

I should of told you how beautiful our baby was. They gave him to me to hold. "Leave you alone for a minute, sir," they said. "Our deepest sympathies." I wanted to shake him, bite him, stick his head under a cold water tap. And rage at the doctor, rage at God – Why? At you, too, Sonia – "I can do something about it." What? What the hell did you do?

But I got down on my knees on the labour ward white-tile floor and rocked him in my arms. His naked little brown body so perfect, his head like a cricket ball in my hand, tiny fingers and toes, his penis smaller than my thumbnail, eyes shut like he sleeping, but still, so still. "Gentle Jesus, take this child of yours, take him home." I put him on the hard iron hospital bed, tucked in the white sheet under his chin so I couldn't see his body turning blue and kissed his forehead. "May the angels protect and keep you, Little Ben."

They asked me if they should take care of the body. Take care – burn him, is what they meaning – more double-talk, like still born. I couldn't think, and your screams telling me no way you could take on a funeral. Me neither, in truth, not then. But now I know we should of had one, whatever kind you wanted, with the Lord's Prayer or not, for *Acceptance*. And we would have a grave with a marble headstone, somewhere we could go with a toy, or a baby book, or a blue flower.

I had nothing to give you – not a hair from his head, not a nail clipping, not a fingerprint.

———

As man, I had to stay strong for you, my heart lock up tight-tight.

But now I am accepting my own grief. I shut the apartment windows so I can't hear the car horns, screeching brakes and the sirens. I draw the thick, green curtains to block the headlights swinging 'cross the ceiling. So quiet, the only thing I can hear is the kitchen clock and the ringing in my ears. I fix a glass of water and sit at the kitchen table with my Bible. But it could be any book with plenty pages 'cause I not reading it, just turning them pages with my eyes closed, one page for every ten ticks of the clock.

First, I let myself see him like a comma inside you, growing arms and legs with his hands waving and his head turning to look at me. I hear his first cry of life, our little wonder-boy. Then I push myself to bathe him with my arm curling under him, and I ease back his foreskin, real gentle, like the books say. I feed him with his special spoon with the plastic tip and lift him up against my shoulder and stroke his back. I watch him roll over, sit up, and we crawl on the living room carpet with me yapping like a puppy, and I show him how to go down our front steps safe – backwards on his hands and knees. I lie with him sleeping on my chest. And I breathe in his baby smell and sing low, *There's a friend for little children above the bright blue sky.*

I push and push some more and take him to Sunday school, in his little blue suit, waistcoat and tie, black shoes shiny. And we go to the sea and he holding my hand and skipping beside me along the sand. And I push one last step and let him speak.

"Daddy, why God made the sky blue?"

"Because He likes blue."

"Better than brown?"

"Well, I don't think we want a brown sky."

"So why he didn't make me blue?"

Until I can take no more. And one day, Sonia, maybe I will tell you this.

I used to snap shut the Bible, drop it like a hot coal, go out on the roof deck and do push-ups and jumping jacks until I half-dead. But these days, I hold strain, mark the page and mark time, the clock ticking on. I used to pray and pray for the answer, but there is no answer. We will never know why, and I trying to reach

to where I don't have to know. I sip the water. Halfway through
the Bible now and, if I get to the end, and got to start again, so be
it.

I see my future walking in front of me, my one, alone. Sonia,
I can't do this without you.

———

Tonight, I turn the pages and think of you – your body, size
twelve, your breasts, size 34B, your feet, shoe size six, three-inch
heels; how you like dark chocolate and how you so frighten for
black dogs; how you like to fix dates and times, and multi-tasking
like you young people say. But I don't know the *you* inside you.
I see you like I did that morning when you thought I did sleeping,
with a pillow up you nightdress and I don't understand why you
grieving so sad and so angry, and so hurtful with no ending.

I close the Bible. It cold tonight so I wrap myself in Mrs. Flynn
white duvet and go out on the roof deck. I see you curl-up in bed
and hear you moaning. I hold you and carry you in his blue
bedroom – you must keep it blue. We do the ABC, put colour
shapes in slots and read stories. And when we can't take no more,
we pack up the toys and the books.

Forget the stages of grief, my love. We will get through, our
own way.

We lie together outside, in the hammock. "Pick a star," I say,
"our Little Ben." And I tell you that you are my silver star and I am
the night sky for you to shine bright again. I look for you to make
mock-sport, but you eyes smiling. I curl 'round you back and
smell the vanilla shampoo. I hold you breasts, lighter now and so
soft. "Sonia, my only love, you got to believe this new kind of
stillness."

I make it so real I reach out to the empty space beside me.

ABOUT THE AUTHOR

Christine Barrow was born in the UK, and has lived in Barbados for nearly fifty years where she worked as an academic in Caribbean Social Development at the University of the West Indies. Since retirement as Professor Emerita, she has participated in creative writing courses. She also attended the 2010 Cropper Foundation Writer's Workshop in Trinidad and Tobago, and the 2015 Callaloo Creative Writing Workshop in Barbados.

She received an Honourable Mention in the 2016 Frank Collymore Literary Endowment Competition, and her work has been published in *Bim: Arts for the 21st Century*, *Poui: The Cave Hill Journal of Creative Writing*, *The Caribbean Writer*, and *Callaloo*. Her story "Panama Man", was short-listed in the 2015 Small Axe Literary Competition, and "He Dances" was awarded Bronze in the 2016 Barbados National Independence Festival of Creative Arts (NIFCA) Literary Competition.

Since retiring Christine Barrow has returned to live in the UK, in Brighton.